The Night Before Scandal

Heart's Temptation Book Seven

By
Scarlett Scott

The Night Before Scandal
Heart's Temptation Book Seven

All rights reserved.
Copyright © 2018, 2019 by Scarlett Scott
Published by Happily Ever After Books, LLC
Print Edition

ISBN: 978-1-095195-84-0

Edited by Grace Bradley
Cover Design by Wicked Smart Designs

This book or any portion thereof may not be reproduced or used in any manner whatsoever without the express written permission of the publisher except for the use of brief quotations in a book review.

The unauthorized reproduction or distribution of this copyrighted work is illegal. No part of this book may be scanned, uploaded, or distributed via the Internet or any other means, electronic or print, without the publisher's permission. Criminal copyright infringement, including infringement without monetary gain, is punishable by law.

This book is a work of fiction and any resemblance to persons, living or dead, or places, events, or locales, is purely coincidental. The characters are productions of the author's imagination and used fictitiously.

For more information, contact author Scarlett Scott.
www.scarslettscottauthor.com

What happens in a carriage doesn't always stay in a carriage

Lord Harry Marlow reluctantly attends a Christmas house party hosted by his brother and his sister-in-law, who also happens to be the woman he once longed to wed himself. He's not pleased by the prospect of holly and mistletoe and merrymaking any more than he is with the reminder of the love he could have had. But his dismay doesn't last for long when a mysterious stranger in the midst of a blizzard captures his interest.

Lady Alexandra Danvers is unabashedly eccentric. Nothing and no man interests her more than her scientific pursuits. Until she meets the sinfully handsome Lord Harry, that is. When sparks fly between the unlikely pairing, scandal isn't far behind. Will Lord Harry and Lady Alexandra find true love together by Christmas day?

Chapter One

December, 1884

THE LAST TIME Lord Harry Marlow had been at Boswell Manor, his brother stole the woman he loved and made her his wife. Fitting, then, that when he returned, Oxfordshire was colder than Wenham Lake ice and the skies had opened to unleash a torrent of snow.

Even more fitting that his carriage suffered a broken axle one quarter of the way down the immense drive, leaving him to the indignity of shivering in the misery of winter's chill whilst his driver walked to the main house for assistance. There was no hope for it. His pride would not allow another moment of cowering like a frightened child in the night calling for his mother.

He threw open the coach door. A squall of white buffeted him, frigid air and snowflakes gusting into his face in further affront. Harry had never cared for either winter or Christmas because he detested being cold as much as he loathed disappointment. Why the hell had he consented to attend this cursed house party?

Icy pinpricks fell down the neck of his coat as he alighted from the carriage with a scowl at the offending heavens, which had not possessed the decency to stave off this ridiculous blizzard until he had been ensconced in the comfort and warmth of Boswell House.

He shook his fist at the sky. "Could this not have waited, damn it?"

"Is berating the clouds an effective method of persuading them to cease precipitation?"

The soft query had him spinning on his heel in the snow.

A fresh gust of wind obliterated his view of the interloper beyond a tall form in bulky trousers, a hat, and a shapeless overcoat. He blinked snowflakes from his lashes. Either his eyes or his ears deceived him, for the voice he'd heard had been distinctly feminine and husky, but the figure before him was completely outfitted in men's garb.

"I beg your pardon?" he demanded, for he did not like being spied upon any more than he liked the prospect of sharing a Boswell Manor Christmas with his brother and sister-in-law and their nauseating love.

As an MP dedicated to his office, Harry liked to think that he was above the too-human emotion of jealousy. But he was a mere mortal after all, and the roiling in his gut and the dread clenching his chest as the carriage had plodded onward to Oxfordshire proved his deficiency.

It wasn't that he was incapable of feeling happy for Spencer. His brother had been through hell and he deserved happiness more than anyone. But a small, unworthy part of Harry could not seem to stop wishing Spencer had discovered that happiness with someone other than the lady *he* had been courting.

His unwanted companion plowed toward him through the snow. There was no other way to describe the person's awkward locomotion. "Awfully arrogant of you to attempt to berate the sky, is all," said the dulcet voice.

Definitely female. As she shuffled toward him in a gait that suggested her boots were at least two sizes too large for her, his curious gaze settled upon a creamy oval face framed by wisps of copper curls. Wide, blue eyes stared at him. Cold tinged her high cheekbones pink. She wasn't beautiful in the conventional sense, but even in her bizarre, mannish dress, there was something arresting about her. Something intriguing.

Best to purge that thought at once. Banish it so far removed that it could never again emerge. The last time he had been drawn to a woman, it had not ended well, and he had no wish for an encore.

Neither did his heart.

She made a huffing sound in her throat. "Are you addlepated or hard of hearing, sir? I said berating the sky is awfully arrogant."

The preposterous wench was hollering at him, enunciating slowly as if he were incapable of comprehending the Queen's English. As if he were the one who was wearing the garb of the opposite sex and chastising strangers in a bloody blizzard.

He blinked, and an inexplicable urge to nettle her rose within him. "I assure you that I am possessed of both sound intelligence and sound hearing, sir. Equally arrogant of you to attempt to berate a stranger. I do not believe we have met. I am Lord Harry Marlow. What brings you to Boswell Manor?"

"*Sir?*" Her fiery brows furrowed, eyes narrowing on him. "I am a guest, my lord."

A guest? Who was she? He noted that she did not bother to correct his intentional misunderstanding of her sex. It was bloody cold out, but perhaps he could warm himself with some entertainment.

Harry considered her through another gust of wind and snow, noting the stray snowflakes clinging to her full bottom lip. "Devil take it. I don't recall when I last saw such a frightful storm before Christmas. Do you, Mr...?"

"Danvers," she supplied. "The storm is fascinating. It certainly seems to be an aberration, which will prove most useful in my meteorological prognostics map."

The skin over his cheekbones tautened with cold. This creature grew stranger by the moment. "Your meteorological prognostics map, Mr. Danvers?"

"Yes." Her blue eyes burned bright with fervor for her subject, and still she made no effort to correct his assumption. She withdrew a small metal tube from her overcoat. "I'm attempting to observe the snowbands with my spectroscope. I have yet to complete the snow portion of my map, and the timing of this storm is really quite fortuitous."

Despite the chill and the driving squall of precipitation, something warm slid through him. Desire, perhaps. Curiosity, certainly. She looked ludicrous in her too-large men's clothing. Everything emerging from her mouth sounded absurd.

And yet, he was drawn to her. "You are studying the storm?"

Another burst of wind caused a smattering of snowflakes to become caught in her lashes. "Of course. Why else would anyone care to be *en plein air* on a day such as this? Stuff and nonsense. The vigorousness of this particular cloud formation does render it frightfully difficult for one to see."

"Here you are." He took a step closer, reached into his own coat, and extracted a handkerchief, using it to blot the offending snow.

His gloved fingers grazed her cheek. He wished they were bare so that he could test the softness of her skin. A tantalizing trail of freckles scattered over her nose. His gaze slipped to her lush, pink lips topped by a perfect Cupid's bow. The urge to cover that mouth with his surged. He allowed his touch to linger, trailing his fingers down her cheek, to the curve of her jaw.

Her lips parted for a moment, as if she searched for words. "Oh. Thank you, Lord Harry. You are most kind."

Still, he did not withdraw his touch but lingered, staring down at her as a fierce ache settled in his groin. As impossible as it seemed, he wanted this odd woman who dressed as a man and spouted nonsense about the weather. Who spoke with a boldness he had only ever experienced from one woman—Lady Boadicea Harrington, the very woman who had subsequently married his brother.

This was no bloody good.

The jangling of tack and clopping of hooves reached him, reminding him that he stood in the midst of a blizzard and he could not feel his cursed toes. What was he doing lingering in the squall, touching this bizarre creature as though it were his right, standing near enough to her to feel her heat and catch a whiff of orange and bergamot?

He did not even know who she was, beyond her surname. He slid his handkerchief into his jacket pocket and took a step back to restore a proper distance and clear his head of her maddening scent. "Mr. Danvers, it's deuced frigid out here. I hear my replacement carriage arriving. Won't you accompany me up to the house?"

Her brows drew together in a frown. "It wouldn't be proper."

"Not proper?" Harry didn't know why goading the female before him was so bloody entertaining, but it was. And he wasn't ready for it to end just yet. "Why, of course it would be proper, Mr. Danvers. You are a guest of my brother's. I wouldn't dream of allowing you to linger out here all alone to catch your death. Come along, then. It will be just two chaps getting to know each other."

She stared, and he wondered if she would relent and

admit that she was not, in fact, a Mr. Danvers at all. But then she tucked her curious metal tube back into her jacket. "I suppose I ought to return before I am missed."

"You may continue your observations from within Boswell Manor," he said then, surprising himself with the need to extend their interaction. But perhaps he had discovered the distraction that would enable him to survive this Christmas with his brother, dragon of a mother, and his sister-in-law, and that would be the only gift he required this Yuletide. "I know just the place."

Chapter Two

*T*HE MOMENT SHE settled into the carriage across from Lord Harry Marlow, Alexandra knew she had made a terrible mistake. The carriage was warm and cozy, laden with fresh hot bricks and furs for comfort, and its confines were small enough—or perhaps she and Lord Harry's legs combined were *long* enough—that their trouser-clad calves brushed.

Such a strange point of contact to affect one, the lower half of the leg. She could not countenance it. Indeed, she had never, before this very moment, given much thought to the existence of her calf aside from its functional purpose. But with his leg pressed against hers, she could not deny the rush of heat that began in that lone spot and spread, curling through her body like an unwanted flame that settled somewhere between her thighs.

What was it about this man that made her body react in such an odd manner? Being a science-minded lady, she knew her response was natural. But why him?

"Have you lost your tongue, Mr. Danvers?" he asked in his low, butter-smooth tone.

It was a pleasant voice, the sort that felt like crushed velvet to her senses—soft yet almost sinful in its luxurious decadence. She forced her gaze to meet his, recalling that he thought her a gentleman because of her attire.

She ought to have corrected his assumption at once. But she had not because the notion of being a man, even for a fleeting moment, had seemed so alluring in its freedom. And also because she did not wish for her brother and sister-in-law to know she was gadding about in public wearing pilfered trousers, boots, and coat.

Without the snow buffeting her face, she had an unobstructed view of him, and he was even more breathtaking than she had supposed. His eyes were the vibrant green of forest moss. Golden hair peeked from beneath the brim of his hat. He was the sort of handsome that would ordinarily make her want to hide. Fine-looking men made her palms sweat.

"Forgive me, Lord Harry, if I am unfit company," she forced herself to say, striving to keep her voice gruff, all the better to preserve her cover. He had said he would take her to an ideal location for her meteorological observations, and she did not wish for him to rescind the offer. That was the only reason she continued the ruse, she assured herself. "It is merely that I am reviewing my observations in my mind."

What rot, but he needn't know that. In truth, the moment he had alighted from his carriage, tall and lean and shaking his fist at the clouds she was intent upon studying, *he* had been the only object of her observations.

"Your observations," he said, flashing her a charming smile that made her belly perform strange gymnastic feats. "What are they?"

For a moment, she could not breathe, for it was as if he had somehow heard her innermost thoughts. Heat rushed to her cheeks, and she had to look away from him, focusing instead upon the snow clinging to her stolen boots.

"Mr. Danvers?" he prodded. "I confess I am quite fascinated by your studies. The instrument you showed me, for instance. What does one use it for?"

Ah. Thankfully, mind-reader was not one of his talents.

She glanced back up at him, reminding herself that she was not Lady Alexandra Danvers in this stolen moment but Mr. Danvers, a gentleman who could do and say as he wished. A gentleman who would decidedly not be dazzled by Lord Harry's golden beauty. There was no need to be shy or nervous. She could simply be herself, embracing all her oddities.

"My spectroscope, you mean, my lord?" She extracted it from her pocket, holding it up for his inspection. "It is ordinarily used to observe rainbands. You simply hold it to your eye and settle it just above the horizon. Most do not believe a spectroscope can be used to predict snowfall because cold air makes the band difficult to see."

He leaned forward, his eyes glittering with something she couldn't define. "May I see it, Danvers?"

"I suppose so." With reluctance, she handed the small instrument over to him. "Do be gentle. There is a compound prism at the end that is easily broken."

As he took it from her, their gloved fingers brushed. "Fascinating," he said, but he wasn't looking at the spectroscope at all.

He was looking at her.

Or, more specifically, at her mouth.

Her lips burned as if he'd touched them, and she wetted them with her tongue. Perhaps she had caught frostbite and that was the reason for the sting. She fought for something to say. "It…it is a unique tool, my lord."

"It is that, indeed." He turned his attention to the spectroscope in his hands at last, turning it this way and that. "You mentioned a map earlier."

"Yes." More heat crept to her cheeks. This was the sort of thing she was not meant to mention in mixed company. But if she was Mr. Danvers, she could say anything, could she not? "I'm making my own diagram that will aid in predicting the weather. Or at least, that is the intended outcome of my efforts."

Thus far, she had not garnered much success. It was only one quarter complete.

"Predicting the weather is a passion of yours?"

What was it about the word "passion" in his silken baritone that made a frisson of something wicked slide down her spine? She stared at him, her gaze absorbing his sculpted lips, the well-defined philtrum, sharp cheekbones, and wide jaw. How could it be that even his nose was perfectly suited to his face? It ought to be a sin for a man to be as compelling as Lord Harry Marlow.

"Danvers?" A knowing grin curved the lips she'd just been ogling.

Heavens. She was making a fool of herself. "It is a passion of mine, yes."

"A man of science," he drawled, shifting his leg so that it brushed against hers in a delicious friction not once but twice. "How intriguing."

She swallowed. Was it just her imagination, or had the carriage air gone stifling? And why did Lord Harry's every action and glance seem to vibrate with a hidden meaning? Good Lord, was this how men spoke to one another in private? Perhaps Lord Harry was the sort of man who enjoyed the company of other men. She wasn't supposed to know of such things, but inquisitive minds had a way of discovering a wealth of information.

The thought successfully quelled any unwanted ardor flaring up within her, for the realization meant he was not interested in Lady Alexandra Danvers at all, but in Mr. Danvers the gentleman. She could hold no candle to Mr.

Danvers.

Alexandra scooted to the side so that their legs no longer touched. "May I have my spectroscope back, my lord?"

Still grinning, he held it out to her, all whilst moving his leg so that it once more pressed against hers. "Of course, old chap. Here you are."

Old chap.

It was another sobering reminder. She knew she was no great beauty—her younger sister Jo, with her lustrous dark hair and petite form, held that title—but it was rather lowering to realize that a man as dazzling as Lord Harry would not be able to see past her outer trappings to recognize her as female. Was she mannish in appearance?

Tucking her instrument back inside her overcoat, she swiveled to look out the window and ascertain their distance from Boswell House. The imposing edifice loomed ahead, and she guessed they would arrive within the next five minutes. It occurred to her that she could not step down from the carriage dressed as a man before all the guests and servants.

Her sister-in-law Clara would box her ears, and her brother Julian would tan her hide. She had promised to be on her best behavior, but they had not been in residence for one day when she had already managed to steal away dressed in a most inappropriate fashion. Not to mention secreting herself inside a carriage with a man she'd only just met.

A man who had mistaken her for a Mr. Danvers.

"Has something overset you, Danvers?" Lord Harry's voice intruded once more.

She turned back with a jolt as she fell into those vivid emerald orbs. *You have overset me*, she wanted to say. But she could not.

When all else failed, prevarication was the only alternative. "I just recalled that I need to take some additional snowfall measurements. Would you mind stopping the carriage so that I may disembark?"

Lord Harry cocked his head, considering her with a warm regard that seemed to reach beneath her skin and pluck at strings she had not known existed. "I do mind, as it happens. I have already suffered one delay on account of the broken axle. We are nearly at Boswell House now. I am certain that your measurements can be obtained there just as well as anywhere."

Alarm tightened into a knot in her stomach. "Please, Lord Harry. It is imperative that I conduct my measurements here."

"Tell me, Danvers, what has you so concerned?" He sounded amused as he leaned forward and placed his large hand upon her knee. "I have instructed the driver to deliver us to the rear entrance."

She struggled to concentrate on his words. Her heart sped into a gallop. Inside her gloves, her palms went slick with sweat, the comfort of her disguise no longer sufficient to stymy her hated reaction to handsome gentlemen. His thumb stroked over her kneecap in a slow, maddening caress.

Surely he would not touch another gentleman with such familiarity. "The rear entrance?" It would seem that all she could manage was brainless repetition of words he had just spoken.

Wonderful. Could the ground beneath them open to swallow her and put an end to her misery, please?

"Naturally." Still, his hand did not move. Instead, his thumb traced a circle higher, on the beginning of her inner thigh. "I promised to show you the ideal spot for meteorological observations at Boswell House, did I not? If we arrive at the front amidst a great deal of pomp and circumstance, all my good intentions will be waylaid by holly boughs, my terrifying mother, and my brother and his wife."

A hint of bitterness entwined itself in Lord Harry's tone as he completed his sentence, and it did not escape her. Some of the warmth curling through her curdled at the observation. For if there was anything that interested Alexandra as much as science and fact, it was gossip. She knew that reading scandal sheets was not a worthwhile endeavor, but it was her lone vice, and she could not shake it.

Which was why she now recalled in explicit detail the rumor that had so recently circulated regarding Lord Harry's courting of his new sister-in-law, the Duchess of Bainbridge, and how his brother the duke had stolen her from beneath his very nose. After receiving Lord Harry's disconcerting attentions and gawping at his good looks, Alexandra could not fathom anyone choosing the Duke of Bainbridge over the golden lord before her.

And though she knew the duchess well from her work with the Lady's Suffrage Society, she had never dared to ask if the rumors were true. She was often more awkward than a bear in a drawing room, but even Alexandra knew when to keep her mouth firmly shut.

She frowned and removed her leg from Lord Harry's reach. "Is your family not expecting you, my lord?"

He raked her with an intense stare and slid on his squab until he crowded her once more with his large, elegant body and intoxicating presence. "I did not tell them when to expect me, and I was explicit with my driver when he left for a substitute carriage that he was to keep my arrival a secret on account of my wishing to surprise my family."

The explanation sounded like a falsehood and his brooding expression amplified her opinion. For some reason, the thought of him still pining after the lovely Duchess of Bainbridge—who she quite liked—bothered her. Even so, she could not argue with an undetected arrival at the rear of Boswell House, all the better for her to blend into the shadows and return to her chamber before her absence was detected.

"How kind of you to surprise them," she said lamely, for his masculine scent—musk with a hint of lemon—hit her then, and she could not look away from him.

His jaw tightened. "The kindness was not meant for them."

"The rumor is true, then." Alexandra pressed a gloved hand to her mouth, wishing she could recall the guileless statement. She had not intended to speak it aloud, but one of her many faults was an unfortunate inability to filter her thoughts before revealing them.

Lord Harry's entire body stiffened, his eyes darkening. "What is true?"

Oh dear. Now she had angered him. She searched her mind for a plausible retort and found nothing. "That you are in love with your brother's wife."

As the words fell heavy in the charged silence, she suppressed a wince. Referring to such a thing had been not only careless, but cruel on her part. Little wonder Clara despaired of ever finding her a suitable match.

His gaze did not waver but remained trained upon her. If anything, the intensity in the luminous depths of his eyes increased. Before she could form a defense, he leaned forward and bracketed her hips in a firm grip, sliding her across the waxed leather of her squab in one swift tug. Their legs tangled, one of his inserted between hers.

She gasped at the suddenness and indecency of the position both. "Lord Harry."

Another tug from him and her bottom no longer rested on her seat at all but upon his hard thigh. His heat burned through her trousers and drawers, searing flesh that came to life, aching with longing. The instinct to grind herself against that rigid thigh was strong. Perhaps this was why women wearing trousers was frowned upon. She could easily see the temptations the freedom of garments encouraged.

And she was grateful for them.

"There is one way to determine whether or not I am," he bit out.

She clutched at his arms, intending to push away from him and return to her side of the carriage. But the muscles beneath her fingers were strong, and at this proximity, his scent was even headier, and his eyes were once again fastened upon her mouth as if it were a feast awaiting a starving man.

Instead of protesting, putting the proper amount of distance between them and turning her mind back to her weather observations where it belonged, she slid forward on his thigh. Just one slow movement that drew her even closer. One pass of her throbbing center over him.

"Damnation, Danvers," he gritted, his hands moving from her hips to her waist, sliding beneath her overcoat and shirt until warm leather caressed bare skin. "Stop moving or we shall both regret what happens next."

She wet her lips, unable to look away, and wondered if she would truly regret it. "I am not a gentleman," she said stupidly.

"I am aware," he growled. "There is nothing manly about you whatsoever. And I'm beginning to think that makes two of us."

His lips were achingly near to hers now. "Two of us?"

"I am no gentleman either, for if I were, I wouldn't do this." His mouth, warm and firm and knowing, claimed hers.

Chapter Three

*T*HE FIRST TOUCH of his lips to hers was nothing short of incendiary. Her mouth was even lusher than it looked. He kissed her with the sudden, voracious hunger that had ignited within him from the moment he'd found himself enclosed in a confined space with her. It was visceral, this need to make his mark upon the strange creature who dressed as a man and spoke of meteorological predictions.

She gasped and he took advantage, his tongue sinking into the wet heat of her mouth. He pulled her closer still, relishing the decadence of her. She tasted like cocoa and sweetness, and nothing and no one had ever been more delicious. He wanted more.

The brim of her hat knocked into his forehead. He plucked it away, tearing his lips from hers so that he could have his first good look at her. She was younger than he had supposed, and he recognized it in the wideness of her eyes, the faultless cream of her forehead. Everything about her was fresh and new and different.

He could say with all honesty that he had never met another woman like her. His gaze swept over the arresting planes of her face, lingering on her freckles, bright-blue eyes, the slight cleft in her chin. Her hair was the lustrous red of a summer sunset, bold and beautiful, gathered into a thick braid that swept down her back. Stray wisps curled around her face.

Harry could not resist catching the tip of his glove in his teeth and shucking it so that he might feel the softness of her skin.

A jolt went through him as his fingers trailed first over her high cheekbone, then lower to the curve of her jaw. She held still for his exploration, eyes never wavering from his. The way she watched him—one part meticulous calculation, one part wary desire—was enough to make his cock twitch. Orange and bergamot perfumed the air. Her thighs clenched around his, and he swore he could feel the molten heat of her cunny through the layers of trousers separating them.

"Your name," he said, striving to keep the breathlessness from his voice lest she think he was so affected by a mere kiss and a woman on his lap. Which of course he was. "Give me your name."

He trailed a caress down the smooth line of her throat, absorbing the wild flutter of her pulse in the hollow at the base. Her coat gaped and he made the tantalizing discovery that her shirt was not buttoned to the collar, leaving a mouthwatering swath of her skin revealed. A wildness took hold.

Just when he thought she would remain stubborn and deny him, she made a hum of pleasure and clutched at his shoulders. "Alexandra."

"Alexandra." He tried it on his tongue, mesmerized by the hitch in her breath as his fingers traced the vee of bare skin he had uncovered. His mind tried to recall an Alexandra Danvers and could not. He was sure he had never met her, and though her name held a certain familiarity, placing it escaped his lust-addled mind.

There were a thousand and one reasons why he ought not to continue on the ruinous path upon which he found himself. A myriad of reasons why he should instead button up her shirt, tug her overcoat about her shoulders, and deliver her to the squab opposite him where she belonged. A whole host of reasons why he should avoid ever setting his lips to hers again.

But Harry had been doing what he should do for his entire life, and all it had managed to get him was the woman he'd wanted to make his wife as his sister-in-law and an interminable Christmas at home looming ahead like a veritable Yuletide gallows. He had worked hard to become an MP, to further his causes and beliefs. His every action had been steeped in caution and precision, designed to uphold the Marlow family name and legacy.

What was the harm in one moment of madness? In giving in to his impulses and desires for the five minutes remaining in the carriage ride to the rear entry of Boswell House? Outside, snow swirled and covered the land in gleaming white. If any holiday was one of endless hope and possibility, surely it was Christmas.

He plucked a button from its mooring. Would it be wrong to see the curve of one ivory breast? Lord Harry Marlow, MP, would never act with such a rash dearth of honor. But that man, the unquestionable gentleman who was always above reproach and did the right thing—the man who had never even once kissed the woman he'd been courting—had grown restless and bored. Yes, he was feeling decidedly out of sorts, and staid, responsible Lord Harry Marlow, MP, could bloody well sod off.

Was this not the season for miracles?

"Lord Harry," she said, stilling his fingers in the act of undoing another fastening on her shirt.

Devil take it. He had gone too far. In a burst, his conscience returned to him, along with the weighty manacles of responsibility. The repercussions for such an indiscretion as this were endless. What in the hell was he doing?

"Forgive me," he forced himself to say, though stopping and forgiveness were the last things he wished to think about in this crazed moment of uninhibited passion.

Had he truly been attempting to debauch an innocent—and one of his family's Christmas guests at that—in a carriage in the midst of a blizzard? He ought to leap from the vehicle and bury his head in the nearest snow bank in shame. He withdrew his touch and clamped his hands around her waist, intending to deposit her safely back on the cushion opposite him.

"My lord, stop," she startled him by ordering in a rather commanding voice for a lady so young. A bewitching flush crept over her cheeks. "Please, would you kiss me again?"

Her sweet request undid him. A bolt of pure, molten lust made his cock go rigid. He went mindless, a growl tearing from his throat as he covered her kiss-swollen lips with his. He had never before seen a female in trousers, but he wholeheartedly approved of her unorthodox decision as his hands swept down to clasp the delicious curves of her hips. There was no mistaking her femininity. She was all woman, lush and lovely.

Her arms twined about his neck, and she scooted nearer on his thigh. The friction of her on his leg unleashed a fresh onslaught of need as the movement crushed her breasts flush against his chest. Her overcoat had done a great deal of concealing.

His tongue dipped once again between her lips, sliding inside her silken heat, and she tasted every bit as sweet as before. His hands seemed to take on a life of their own, clawing at her overcoat, peeling away her layers until he palmed the heavy weight of her breasts through her shirt. She did not wear a corset, and her hard nipples prodded him in reward. Every part of her, from the breathy sighs she made to the way she ground against him, to the pebbled peaks of her breasts, was so responsive.

She was a fierce thing, and he was drawn to her heat, to her flame.

For the first time in his life, the prospect of getting burned didn't alarm him.

Nothing alarmed him other than the thought of having to end their kiss, which surely he must. The carriage had ceased to sway. Either they were once more lodged in the snow with yet another broken axle for their efforts, or they had reached their destination.

But he could not seem to control himself. His thumbs rubbed over the tight buds of her nipples in slow circles. He sucked her lower lip into his mouth, dragged kisses over her jaw, pressed his lips to the shell of her ear, traced its delicate whorl with his tongue until she shivered.

His blood thundered through his veins, and all he knew was that he had to have this woman. He kissed Alexandra's throat, inhaled deeply of her scent, for it seemed concentrated on the smooth dip of skin where her shoulder and her neck met.

The urge to taste her here would not be contained. He opened his mouth and sucked her skin, wringing a moan from her. She tasted of orange and the saltiness of her skin and something else that was indefinable yet delicious. Harry plucked at her nipples, emboldened by her response, half drunk on the way she made him feel—as if he were simultaneously high in the clouds and weightless, capable of all things, wild and free.

He never wanted this moment of abandon to end.

And then it did.

The door to the carriage was wrenched open without warning, and a blast of frigid air, a wall of snow, and a chorus of shocked gasps invaded the sheltered cocoon of the carriage.

"Unhand my sister, Marlow!"

The irate masculine voice cut through the haze of lust infecting his mind more effectively than cold, snowflakes, or scandalized murmurings ever could. It was a voice he recognized, and suddenly the pieces of the puzzle came together in perfect synchronicity.

Alexandra Danvers.

Lady Alexandra Danvers, to be precise. Sister to one Julian Danvers, reformed rake, formidable pugilist, and the Earl of Ravenscroft.

He tore his mouth from Alexandra's throat, dread supplanting all lust, reason crowding all longing. Lord Harry Marlow, MP, returned to his senses to find a bevy of shocked faces gawping into the carriage and a thoroughly enraged Earl of Ravenscroft crowding the exit. In a moment of stinging clarity, he noted his mother's pinched face, his brother and sister-in-law gaping in shock, and his mother's bosom bow—and most reprehensible gossip in all England—the Duchess of Cartwright wide-eyed and sharp-eared.

Bloody hell.

He thrust Lady Alexandra back onto her squab as though she were made of flame, dragging a hand over his mouth. It was no use. The evidence of what he'd been about could not be hidden. Nor could he extricate himself from this farce without making reparations.

What had he done?

"What have you done?"

Alexandra winced as her brother, who she had—until the last hour, or so—considered the great scapegrace of the family, bellowed the question at her in outrage.

They were seated in one of Boswell House's many salons. It was a putrid shade of green, filled with an alarming amount of gilt, and hung with an array of boring oil pastorals. She was still, most regrettably, wearing the overcoat, shirt, trousers, and boots she had stolen from him. Rather disconcerting for any attempts to defend one's self. How could she claim innocence when she wore the evidence of her sins?

And she wasn't talking about the marks Lord Harry's wicked mouth had left upon her skin, evidenced by the reflection she'd glimpsed in a looking glass hung in the labyrinth of halls. The red marks on her throat both shocked and intrigued her. She had not known a gentleman could possess such ardor. Now that she did...

"Damn it, Alexandra, you will answer me or I will bury you in the country for the next three years at bloody minimum," Julian growled at her, stalking toward her with a menacing air that did not frighten so much as it dismayed.

She loved her older brother dearly, and the knowledge that she was cause for his disappointment lodged in her belly like a leaden weight. He knew how much she detested the country. That he would issue such a threat now spoke to his outrage.

Outrage which was, admittedly, understandable. She had been discovered dressed in scandalous fashion, riding Lord Harry Marlow's thigh as if he were her trusted steed whilst he feasted upon her neck and visited the most exquisite torture upon her breasts. Just thinking about it now made warmth bloom between her thighs and the scalding heat of embarrassment color her cheeks. How had she allowed such a thing to happen?

Also, how had she not realized such wonders existed?

"Alexandra Maria Danvers, I expect a response," her brother prodded, his tone no less furious. "You will give me your explanation for the outrage that I and almost *all the other guests* assembled beneath this roof just witnessed."

She pursed her lips, considering how she ought to respond. Her brother was no stranger to sins, having spent the years before his marriage to Clara cultivating his reputation for debauchery. "As you know, I am crafting a meteorological prognostics map."

He stalked back across the salon, raking a hand through his hair. "I am aware. What I find myself pondering is what in the name of God meteorology has to do with Lord Harry Marlow mauling you in a carriage whilst you are dressed as a man." He paused, his lip curling as he raked her from head to toe with a blistering glare. "Wearing my damned clothing, no less."

She frowned. "Lord Harry was not mauling me, Julian. Pray do not be so melodramatic."

Her brother's brows snapped together, his mien turning ferocious. "He *was* mauling you, damn it, and anyone with eyes in their head witnessed it. Jesus Christ, Alexandra, you have not even had your comeout yet."

No, she had not, but not because she was not of an age. Her brother's dubious reputation and antics both had left her and her younger sister Josephine in the care of an elderly aunt until her brother's nuptials. And then Julian had insisted upon further tutelage in the finer arts of being a proper lady before allowing her presentation.

Clearly, it had not done her a lick of good.

But what did he expect? They were cut from the same wicked cloth. Their mother had bedded so many men that no one knew the identities of their fathers. Almost certainly, none of them had been the issue of the departed Earl of Ravenscroft, Julian included.

She took a breath, uncertain of how to proceed but following her instinct. "Julian, I was conducting measurements and attempting to observe the snowbands when Lord Harry's carriage suffered a setback. A new carriage arrived to carry him the rest of the way to Boswell House, and he was gracious enough to take me with him so that I did not need to tramp through the growing snowfall alone. It was most gentlemanly."

In truth, nothing about the time she'd spent in Lord Harry Marlow's intoxicating presence had been gentlemanly or proper. From the moment their gazes had first clashed, even through the pelting snowfall, she had felt something deep and smoldering and true arcing between them. His emerald gaze had been too knowing, too bold. His words, his every observation and caress and kiss...good heavens, she had not known such potent persuasion existed. It was as if he had somehow been fashioned precisely for her, and she for him.

The rational, science-minded part of her would have scoffed at such a notion as a flight of fancy had she not just experienced it for herself. She wanted to know him intimately, and she already mourned the loss of his touch.

"Gentlemanly?" her brother demanded, so loudly and with such disbelief that she flinched.

She wished he would cease stalking about and sit down to engage in a civilized discourse, but this was Julian, and he was a law unto himself. Alexandra sighed. "Please do calm yourself, brother dearest. You are hollering so loudly that I have no doubt the gossipmongers can hear you in London."

"They will have already heard by now anyway thanks to the accommodating tongue of the Duchess of Cartwright," he snapped. "Have you any idea the hounds of hell you have just unleashed upon us all? That woman is the most notorious gossip in the *ton*. Have no doubt that she will take everything she witnessed today straight to the waiting ears of anyone who will listen. You have ruined yourself before you have even made your bloody curtsy."

When he phrased it that way, she supposed she ought to be concerned. But his dire words prompted no such sentiment. Indeed, she felt nothing more than a buoying sense of relief, for her unprecedented reaction to Lord Harry aside, she did not want to wed. "She may tell anyone she likes anything she desires. I have no wish to marry anyone, Julian, and I have been telling you so for months now."

"Nonsense," he said curtly, pinning her with a bright-blue glare. "You are too damn young to know what you want. When the time comes, you will wish for a man who loves you, for a marriage and children."

Her sister-in-law Clara was increasing, and Alexandra was reasonably certain impending fatherhood was rotting her brother's brain. "I do not need a man who loves me or marriage and children to satisfy me. I am a woman of science. I can be happy as I am, studying the weather and drafting my prognostics map."

Julian's strides ate up the distance between them until he towered over her. "Apparently not, sister dearest, else you would not have been acting with such rash disregard for propriety in a carriage with Lord Harry. I will own the blame for your moral failings, since God knows I've more than my fair share. It cannot have been easy having me for a brother. But by God, Alexandra, this sort of thing…it is beyond the pale, and the only way it can be rectified is through marriage."

She stilled, for she did not care for the sudden trajectory of their conversation. "Marriage?"

Her brother's expression hardened. "I did not wish this for you, but I'm afraid you've left me with no choice. You must wed Lord Harry. After I deliver a sound trouncing to him, of course."

Alexandra shot from her seat. "There will be no marriage and there will be no trouncing, Julian. I will not be forced into a lifelong sentence with a man I scarcely know."

Julian's gaze was harsh, his jaw hard. "You damn well should have considered your lack of acquaintance before allowing him liberties."

Shame curdled her stomach. She still did not know what madness had overcome her. Had it been the dizzying sense that she and Lord Harry were the only two people in the world for that brief interlude in the carriage with snow falling all around them? Had it been the false sense of freedom afforded her by dressing as a man?

She reached for her brother's arm, laying a staying hand upon it and absorbing the tenseness in his bearing. "I am sorry, Julian. It was not my intention to cause such a kerfuffle."

"This is not a kerfuffle, Alexandra." His voice remained curt, his expression impassive. The pensive man before her was not the warmhearted, yielding brother she knew. "This is a scandal in the making, the life-altering sort which neither you nor I nor Josephine can afford. And I have not even begun to address the matter of your thievery."

She bit her lip. "What you call thievery I prefer to think of as well-intentioned borrowing."

"Semantics," he hissed, refusing to bend. "Damn it, you cannot run about the grounds of the Duke of Bainbridge's estate wearing clothes you stole from me, and you most certainly cannot closet yourself in an enclosed carriage with his brother and allow the bastard to dishonor you."

Well. When he phrased her actions in such succinct fashion, she could not offer an argument, could she? It was all true. She was a horrid sister. Julian was in the midst of polishing his tarnished reputation with Clara at his side, and her younger sister Jo could also be tainted by her carelessness.

If only Julian and the other guests had not chosen to venture into the snow for an ice-skating party. As if such a thing was to be even entertained in such a downfall…

She relented, the severity of her actions hitting her with the force of a smack to the cheek. Julian was correct. The gathering may be a relatively intimate one by country house party standards, and the Christmas season may be one of gaiety and frivolity, but she *had* been caught wearing men's clothing while sitting upon the lap of Lord Harry Marlow, who had been doing an admirable job of ravishing her mouth.

Her lips still tingled to think of those kisses, which had been nothing short of wondrous. And her breasts, oh how they ached with a strange new need at the memory of his thumbs working over her nipples. She had not known her flesh could be brought to life in such a fashion. For the whole of her days, she had believed her body to be a thing of utility, each part crafted for a specific purpose. Her mouth to obtain sustenance, her breasts to feed a babe one day should she have one, her legs to enable her to walk, her ears to hear, etcetera.

But Lord Harry Marlow had proven her wrong with one stolen interlude in a carriage, and now she could not seem to quell the fever he had given her.

This would not do. She took a deep, fortifying breath and focused on the most troubling aspect of her indiscretions. "I am wholeheartedly sorry if my actions cause harm to you or Josephine in any fashion, Julian. You must believe it is the last thing I would ever wish. I love you both, and I would never intentionally hurt either of you."

"Then you will marry Lord Harry, and the sooner the better," came her brother's frosty, unwanted response.

"He has not offered for me," she protested.

Julian flashed a chilling smile. "I will assist him in rectifying that matter."

"No violence," Alexandra was compelled to order him. "Please. And moreover, I do not wish to marry."

Julian sighed then, passing a hand over his face. The gesture left him looking weary and resigned. "You forfeited your choice in the matter when you went into that carriage, Lex. It's my duty as your brother to see this through now."

Panic sliced through her, dispelling the ridiculous flights of fancy that sought to dwell upon the way Lord Harry made her feel. She clutched her brother's sleeve ever tighter. "Please, Julian. You cannot mean to force me."

He covered her hand, his countenance turning grim. "There will be no need to force you. You will do what you must to preserve your good name and keep from harming Josephine's chances for a future match both. Return to your chamber now, and I will meet with Lord Harry."

The panic turned to dread and then an icy sense of understanding and impending doom. Julian was right. If Lord Harry offered for her, she would have no choice but to accept his hand and marry a man she scarcely knew.

"No fisticuffs, Julian," she begged. "Please."

Her brother raised a haughty brow. "I make no promises on that score. If the man requires a thrashing, then a thrashing he shall receive."

"But it is Christmastime, and we are guests of the duke. Surely it would be ill-mannered of you to pummel his brother into wedding me?" she pressed, unable to adhere to his wishes and disappear until she had reassurance. The thought of Julian and Lord Harry facing each other like a pair of pugilists disturbed her.

Julian shook his head, his expression revealing nothing. "No more protests, imp. Go to your chamber. You've caused enough troubles to last us for the next five Yuletides at least."

Yes, she supposed she had. Feeling suddenly as weary as her brother looked, she yielded. As she took her leave of the chamber, a new determination soared through her. She would find a way to extricate herself from this mess. A way that did not involve a hasty marriage to Lord Harry Marlow.

For as lovely as his kisses were and as maddening as his caresses, she had matters to concern her that were of far greater import than any gentleman could ever be. She had no wish to be tied down and married to any man. Some time ago, she had decided to devote herself to two causes: gaining the vote and science. Her actions today had been an aberration.

One she had no intention of repeating.

Chapter Four

"BLOODY HELL, HARRY, you're going to have to marry the girl," clipped his brother, every bit the icy Duke of Bainbridge.

Seated opposite Spencer in his study, Harry tossed back a hearty gulp of whisky. Yes, he was going to have to marry Lady Alexandra Danvers. For some reason, the realization did not disturb him nearly as much as it ought. As a fledgling MP, the scandal he'd just created should be enough to chill him to his core. Add to that the fact that the lady in question was not only eccentric but was the sister to the notorious Earl of Ravenscroft and any man worth his salt would be quaking in his boots.

Perhaps it was the liquor or perhaps it was a stupor of a different variety entirely, but Harry could not shake the incipient burst of anticipation within him. More of Lady Alexandra's lush mouth, her delectable body his to discover and pleasure, did not fill him with trepidation. Instead, it imbued him with an odd surge of expectation.

"I will do my duty, Spencer," he assured his brother. "Of that you need have no doubt."

Spencer skewered him with an assessing look. "If you don't mind my asking, what in the hell were you thinking? Mother nearly had an apoplectic fit."

He slanted a narrow-eyed glare back. "Mother should be

accustomed to scandal, having one son whose life has been the embodiment of it, no?"

His brother stiffened, his jaw hardening. "Harry, if this is about Boadicea, you could have damn well left an innocent out of it."

"It is not," he was swift to insist, for Lady Alexandra had nothing to do with his former infatuation with his sister-in-law.

With time, distance, and love for his brother, Harry had realized that Boadicea was a far better match for Spencer than she would have been for himself. She had brought his brother out of his self-imposed exile and had introduced much-needed joy back into his life. For those reasons, Harry was grateful. To suggest that his attraction—and resulting indiscretion—with Lady Alexandra had been caused by his unrequited attachment to Boadicea was inherently wrong.

Spencer was quiet, studying him in a way that made Harry shift in his chair and take another swig of his whisky. Apparently, he approved of what he saw, for he gave a nod at last. "Very well. I think Lady Alexandra will be good for you. Did I not warn you that one day you would find the woman who would drive you to distraction? It would seem we have arrived at that day far sooner than either you or I could have imagined."

"You also told me never to settle for anything less," he pointed out with a sardonic air he could not quite suppress. "A forced marriage to save two reputations seems to be rather a sort of settling, does it not?"

"Not necessarily," his brother said, taking a sip of his own whisky at last. "If you will recall, my nuptials with Boadicea occurred in much the same manner. Think of it this way, if you will. There are any number of ladies with whom you could have caused a scandal over the years and any number of indiscretions in which you could have indulged. This one was different, and there is a reason for that."

Yes, this one was different. *She* was decidedly different. Lady Alexandra Danvers, who gadded about in men's garb, who was compiling a weather prognosticator, who carried about a tool to measure rain and snowbands in her pocket. Who had flaming red hair, bewitching freckles, a lush mouth he could not help but kiss, and the most deliciously curved breasts, waist, and hips he had ever set his hands upon...that Lady Alexandra Danvers was unlike any other female he had ever known.

And in a decidedly good way.

She was refreshing, vexing, confusing, and alluring all at once. He could not get enough of her. She frightened the hell out of him. But all the same, he could not stop wanting her. Perhaps Spencer was not that far from the mark, and she was the woman who would indeed drive him to distraction.

What then? Would it be so indecent to want her? Would it be so injudicious to make her his?

"You are not wrong," he conceded. "Lady Alexandra is the only lady with whom I desire to begin a scandal. As foolish and impossible as it seems, it is nevertheless truth."

The stark, unmistakable sound of a fist pummeling the door of the study interrupted the peaceful exchange just then. There was precious little finesse on the part of whomever happened to be on the opposite side of the portal. If Harry had to hazard a guess as to the perpetrator, he would place his coin upon the Earl of Ravenscroft.

"Bainbridge, Marlow, I know you are within," came a muffled but outraged voice through the portal. "Do I need to break down the bloody door, or will you invite me in?"

Spencer eyed him, ill-concealed amusement curving his lips into a half smile. This sudden propensity for levity—

previously absent from his brother's mien—Harry blamed upon his sister-in-law Boadicea as well.

"All set to rampage, is he not?" Spencer asked with a guffaw that suggested he was *enjoying* this, the knave. "Perhaps you ought to grant him entrance."

"Enter," he called to the brother of the woman he had just disgraced.

A hopelessly awful situation in which he now found himself. He, Lord Harry Marlow, who had always been above reproach, who had never taken advantage of anyone let alone a defenseless female, who had taken care in his every action, curating his reputation as a gentleman…he was now being forced to marry a woman he hardly knew. All because he had unbuttoned her shirt, teased her nipples, and kissed her as if she were a seasoned courtesan.

He stood and faced Ravenscroft, feeling as if it were pistols at dawn. The earl's expression was hard as granite, his customary unflappable charm nowhere in evidence. He stalked across the study, stopping only when he was close enough to strike. Harry stood tall and braced himself for the blow he knew was coming. Would it be his nose or his chin? Perhaps a blackened eye.

"Bainbridge," the earl greeted Harry's brother first in deference to his rank before turning his glacial gaze upon Harry. His lip curled. "Lord Harry. I do believe felicitations are in order."

"Ravenscroft," acknowledged Spencer in an equally clipped fashion. Their wives were dear friends, and the awkwardness in their manner had to be down to Harry's ignominious presence and actions both.

Felicitations.

Here was the blow, then. Not a fist but the sentence of a lifetime. The earl wanted him to marry Lady Alexandra. Harry waited again for the shock to pierce him like a needle. For his mind to violently balk at the notion of marrying the eccentric younger sister of the notorious Earl of Ravenscroft. For his common sense to recall that the woman who would be his wife wore her oddness like a Worth gown, dressing as a man, creating a weather prognostics map, observing a bloody blizzard as though it were the most natural occupation in the world for a gently bred lady.

Mocking him for berating the sky.

Daring to ask for his kiss.

Being bold and different.

Her sunset hair, those tiny copper specks on her nose, the wide blue eyes, sultry mouth, the perfect handfuls of her breasts…there he went once more, down the garden path. And no matter which way he trod, he could not seem to summon up the dread he ought to be feeling in this moment.

The silence in the study returned him to the present, as did the expectant gazes of his brother and the earl. He blinked, collected himself, focused on Ravenscroft. "Will you grant me your sister's hand then, my lord?"

Ravenscroft's eyes narrowed. "Had you asked me the same query yesterday, and had it been something Lady Alexandra would have wished for herself, I would have answered in the affirmative. After having witnessed your ravishment of my innocent sister not two hours past, I cannot say in good conscience that I will grant you her hand without some reassurance."

Harry forced himself to tamp down his inner outrage at being accused of ravishment, of all the outlandish things. What had occurred in the carriage had been mutual. Not to mention the irrefutable fact that Lady Alexandra herself had asked for his kisses. Yes, he should have exercised caution and restraint, being the older and more experienced gentleman.

But Lady Alexandra Danvers begging for a kiss would tempt the morals of a bloody saint.

And a saint, it was more than apparent, he was not.

He nodded. "Of course, my lord."

"A whisky, Julian?" Spencer interrupted, rising to offer the earl a newly poured glass.

"Hell yes," the earl said with a grimace, before tossing back a gulp of amber-colored liquid. "Fine stuff, old boy. Scottish?"

Spencer inclined his head and raised his own glass in salute. "Naturally."

What a puzzling development. He felt suddenly as if he were an outsider, witnessing the easy camaraderie between Spencer and the earl. His own relationship with his brother had been strained following Spencer's usurping of his intended bride, but they had made amends. And Harry had decided that seeing his brother happy was of far greater import than pride.

Harry frowned. "Forgive me, Lord Ravenscroft, but what manner of reassurance are you requiring to enable me to marry Lady Alexandra?"

The earl took another healthy swig of his whisky. "We are to be in residence at Boswell House for the next fortnight. Court her. *Earn* her hand. Prove to me that you deserve to have her as your wife by Christmas. If she tells me she wishes to wed you at the end of that time, I will be willing to see the two of you wed."

This was decidedly not the response that Harry had anticipated from an outraged brother of a female who had just been compromised. In truth, what he had imagined—what he deserved—was a sound trouncing. At the very least a bloodied nose.

What was he meant to say? That he deserved to have

Alexandra as his wife when he knew damn well that he didn't? That he would earn her hand and prove himself when he was also sure that he couldn't?

He finished his own whisky, relishing the burn of it in his gut, for it reminded him of the severity of his actions. "I will do whatever I must. The scandal of today cannot withstand anything less than Lady Alexandra becoming my wife. Surely you must realize that, my lord."

Ravenscroft was bloody addlepated if he would not accept Harry's suit. He hailed from one of the most distinguished houses in England. He was the son of a duke, an MP, a man of unparalleled reputation—today's scandalous lapse notwithstanding.

The earl raised a brow. "Let me be perfectly candid. I love my sister, and one of my primary charges is to see her happily settled in life with a man who will love and appreciate her precisely as she is. I have yet to decide who that man is. What I witnessed earlier today does not precisely instill a great deal of hope within me for your suitability Marlow, as you must understand."

A surge of guilt hit Harry at the reminder of how egregious his actions had been. "I apologize for my rash behavior."

The earl's gaze was honed as sharp as a dagger. "If you so much as breathe upon her in the wrong way, I shall thrash you into next week. Understood? Observe the damned proprieties, you jackanapes."

Harry gritted his teeth. Yes, he deserved that remonstration. But that didn't mean he could kowtow with ease. "Let us leave it in the lady's hands, shall we? In the interim, I promise to be on my best behavior."

Which had never been a problem before.

Now?

Harry thought of all that creamy skin, those sweet breasts,

the curves of her hips, those hard, responsive nipples. No, there was no way on God's earth that he could promise to be on his best behavior with the luscious and altogether glorious Lady Alexandra Danvers.

Ravenscroft finished his whisky and continued to pin Harry with a glare. "I still want to pummel you, Marlow. Give me a reason. One reason."

"My brother is a paragon," Spencer decided to chime in at that moment, raising his glass toward Harry as if in toast. "He is a good man, and Lady Alexandra could ask for none better in a husband. You will not regret granting him this chance, Julian. Mark my words."

The earl's eyes flitted from Harry to Spencer before settling back on Harry once more. "See that you prove your brother correct, Lord Harry. Otherwise, I seriously doubt your career as an MP can withstand a scandal such as this."

It was a warning.

A reminder.

Harry nodded. He needed neither. For as frightening and unexpected as it was, he had accepted the notion of Lady Alexandra Danvers as his wife. As the mother of his future children. As the woman who would remain forever by his side.

He swallowed. "I will earn Lady Alexandra's hand before Christmas. You have my word."

Ravenscroft grinned, but it held little mirth. "If I don't, you have my fists, Marlow."

Chapter Five

⇶⫷

*T*HE SNOW CONTINUED to fall that evening as the Welcome Ball got underway. Wreaths of fir and holly adorned the walls of the ballroom, faux snow bedecked corners of the floor, and an enormous Christmas tree towered over the procession in glittering majesty. The effect of it all, coupled with the perfectly groomed and coifed lords and ladies spinning about the polished parquet floor, would have taken the breath of most observers.

But Alexandra was not just any observer, and quadrilles did not interest her, nor did flirtations or furtive searches of the sea of faces for Lord Harry Marlow—who had yet to appear. She most certainly was *not* looking for him but her empirical examination had nevertheless noted his absence.

Julian would not have beaten him to a pulp, would he? What if he and Lord Harry had pummeled one another into oblivion? When her brother and his wife had quietly escorted Alexandra and Josephine to the ball earlier, she had not detected any injuries upon his person. But now, her imagination ran wild. She imagined Lord Harry sporting a broken nose and a blackened eye and shuddered.

Heaving another displaced sigh, Alexandra shifted in the corner she presently occupied amidst a grouping of potted holly bushes. Her right foot tapped. Then her left.

Balls were so deadly boring. Such a monumental waste of

one's time and attentions. Why, she could be outside taking hourly measurements and temperature readings and recording the results in her journal. It seemed horridly unfair that she should be denied the opportunity to further her studies for her prediction map.

She had observed the weather all afternoon from the window of her chamber, where she had been promptly banished following her ruination. Forced to relinquish her boots, trousers, shirt, and overcoat, she had remained at the window like a morose sentinel, inwardly bemoaning her fate. But at least she had been able to watch and take notes, to add to her prognostic.

Trapped in the ballroom, she was yet another awkward miss, too tall for fashion, hair an unsightly shade of red, who had somehow been compromised by the Duke of Bainbridge's brother. Oh yes, she had felt the stares.

The gathering was small and select enough that she could flit about with the revelers prior to her comeout, but not everyone here was her friend.

Indeed, most were not. She was aware that she was gauche and odd. That she said and did the wrong things at the wrong times, that she often acted without regard for consequence, and that she was hopelessly inept at behaving as a genteel lady ought.

"Why are you not dancing?"

The voice, butter-rich and deep and so near to her ear that gooseflesh pebbled on her arms, had her jumping and spinning to face its source in a swirl of emerald skirts. There he stood, a few inches taller than she, his golden hair tousled in waves, his green eyes vivid and knowing upon her.

Oh. Thank heavens, he did not appear harmed. He was as handsome as any man she had ever seen. And even more handsome now than he had been earlier in the carriage and snow, resplendent in his formal evening wear. He almost stole all the breath from her lungs.

"Lord Harry," she said, wishing his name did not emerge as a gasp. "I do not dance."

Heavens, put her in a dress, and all the ease with which she had interacted before suddenly dissipated like the clouds after a thunderstorm.

Lord Harry offered her an elegant bow, a boyish smile on his lips. "Danvers. I must admit that the sight of you in a gown is as surprising as it is lovely. Why do you not dance?"

She pursed her lips and studied him, trying to discern if he was teasing her or if he was serious. Perhaps a combination of the two, she decided. "Because I am an abysmal dancer. Monsieur Bouchard, my instructor, despaired of my ineptitude. I drove the poor fellow to tears."

His smile widened, his eyes crinkling at the corners. "Tears, you say? I cannot countenance it."

Alexandra found herself smiling back at him. "The tears may have been because I stomped on his instep after he suggested that I should compensate for the dreadful color of my hair by dancing with the grace of a swan."

Lord Harry's smile fled. "Your hair is glorious. You should have stomped on both his insteps for such an affront."

"One was enough," she assured him, recalling the moment her odious dance instructor had retreated, never to return. "It was a very thorough stomp, and I am no sparrow."

"No indeed," he said somberly, his gaze roaming her face. "If I were to compare you to a bird, it would never be something as boring as a sparrow."

"I would never wish to be a bird," she said with a shudder, "forever winging my way from tree to tree, prey to creatures five times my size. Consuming all my sustenance with a beak. Only think of how tiring it is to be avian. Isn't it odd that

THE NIGHT BEFORE SCANDAL

birds are hatched from eggs? Why, they're almost reptilian in nature, and no one likes snakes."

Oh dear, there she went. Rambling again. Her face went hot. Would she never learn her lesson? She bit her lip to stay additional words that threatened to spill forth like water over a dam. Julian had issued his sentence to her like a jailer. She was to marry Lord Harry Marlow to atone for her sins. However, there had been nary a word of such a thing. During her hours alone in her chamber, she had fretted that a betrothal announcement would occur that very evening at the ball.

And yet, only her sister-in-law Clara had visited her, with a pitying smile, a commiserating embrace, and instructions that she should heed Julian's wishes. Josephine had been kept from her tainted presence altogether until this evening. And Julian had never reappeared until she had been marched in deafening, disappointed silence to the ball.

He had growled a single sentence at her before allowing her to abscond to the fringes of the *fête* as was always her wont. *Do not do anything foolish this evening, Alexandra.*

And truly. Did he expect her to honor that or any other command?

"Would flying to one's destination be such a chore?" Lord Harry asked then, intruding upon her jumbled musings. "Just think of how lovely it would be to soar through the sky."

"Think of how awful it would be to plummet to the earth," she countered, unable to help herself. It was the nature of her brain.

He took a step closer. "Alexandra."

There was undisguised intent in his voice.

Of what, she couldn't be sure. But she felt it in her breasts, the tips tingling and tightening in recollection of the torture his thumb had visited upon them. She felt it in the ache that throbbed between her legs. In the steady sweep of desire that licked down her spine and settled low in her belly.

She swallowed, casting a surreptitious glance around the ballroom. The revelers were all seemingly otherwise engaged, dancing in a swirl of multicolored silks and dark evening wear, the orchestra playing away on their strings. The potted holly and faux snow underfoot gave them the illusion of privacy.

No one was watching.

She swayed toward him before recalling herself. "Lord Harry?"

He touched her chin for a brief moment. Not her jaw, not her throat. It was not a caress but a gentle touch. An affirmation that what they had shared earlier in the carriage had been real, that the connection between them was undeniable. "You are the strangest creature I've ever met."

She stilled, an arrow of hurt somehow zinging its way to her heart. "I will own my strangeness. I would far prefer to be odd than a boring, insipid, brainless female."

He quirked a golden brow, his expression unreadable. "Who said that there is anything wrong with being strange?"

"You, my lord," she said. "Rather, to be more specific, perhaps you implied it."

"I am strange," he surprised her by saying.

"You?" It was impossible to fathom that a man as beautiful and polished as Lord Harry Marlow could possibly be anything less than perfection incarnate.

"Me," he affirmed, taking another step closer until his trousers brushed the fall of her skirts.

"How?" she asked, intrigued. Something inside her sparked to life once more, and it was a different something than the mad, corporal attraction that had flared in the carriage.

He took one more step, and she melted into the potted holly bush at her back. They were effectively shielded from the rest of the ballroom. Somehow, not even the prickly ends of the holly leaves disturbed her. Lord Harry commanded all of her attention.

He dipped his head as though he were imparting a secret of the gravest import. "I do not like fruit."

"That is interesting, my lord," she agreed with a speculative air. "However, it is decidedly not enough to classify you as strange. A great many people dislike various fruits, you must realize."

He pondered her with a grave expression. "*All* fruit, Lady Alexandra?"

She blinked. "Strawberries?"

Lord Harry shook his head. "Too many tiny, irritating seeds."

It was a valid argument, but she was also determined to prove him wrong. "Plums?"

He gave a mock shudder. "Too tart and fleshy."

"Cherries," she said triumphantly.

"Alas, the pit of the cherry comprises at least half its density," he said in a regretful tone. "I cannot appreciate a fruit that is mostly seed."

Was it her imagination at work, or had he stepped closer while she'd been distracted by shuffling through her mind for fruits he could not deny enjoying?

"Oranges?" she asked hopefully.

"I'm afraid the pith and seeds are far too distracting, as is the necessity of peeling to reveal the fruit itself." He shook his head once more. "All that effort for a citrus that is often sour and unworthy."

"The same could be said of most people," she observed before she could stifle her tongue.

"Yes." A sudden, beautiful grin curved his lips then. "Do you know what I like about you, Lady Alexandra?"

Oh dear. She would have retreated farther into her nest of holly, but the prickly thing was already clinging to her silk. Moreover, the last scandal she needed was to topple backward, skirts in the air, into an upended pile of Christmas shrubs. But he was crowding her, and his intimate tone, nearness, and the delicious, masculine scent of him was enough to weaken her every intention to behave as a proper lady ought.

"What do you like about me?" she asked in spite of herself, for he was charming and he was handsome, and he was also different. No gentleman she'd ever met before him had been able to keep pace with her, to navigate the turns and tangents of her mind without pause. Certainly, no man had ever enjoyed it.

His grin softened to an intimate smile, and he brushed a lone finger along her bare collarbone just once, and so quickly that she would have thought she imagined the touch had it not branded her skin like a flame. "I like your quick mind. I like your feistiness. I like the daring that enabled you to traipse about dressed as a gentleman at a house party attended by the most fashionable set in London. I like your bold hair, the sweet trail of freckles on your nose. I like your mouth beneath mine."

"Lord Harry," she protested because she should, and not because he had affronted her. Quite the opposite, for she had never been rendered breathless by a mere handful of sentences before.

"I also like that you say precisely what is on your mind," he continued, "that you don't blunt your opinion by what a lady should say, and that you are refreshingly unique."

She pursed her lips, considering him. "You like that I am strange?"

He captured her gaze, holding it with his, and the fierce light burning within those emerald depths refused to allow her to look away. "I do believe that I like everything about you, Danvers. And I do not think you are strange. I think you are an original. Besides, I already told you my own quirk."

"Disliking fruit is hardly a cross to bear," she pointed out, enjoying herself as she had not done in…well, *ever* in the presence of a gentleman.

Oh, she had relished every one of his skilled kisses and caresses earlier in the carriage, but this matching of wits was a different, more dimensioned level of gratification. He made her melt and he also fed her mind. What a dazzling, troubling, addictive combination.

His mouth quirked. "Become more familiarly acquainted with me. I promise that my dislike of fruit is not my sole oddity."

It was her turn to shake her head, casting a wild-eyed glance over his shoulder to the fraction of the ballroom yet visible to her. Couples paired off. Laughter abounded. Silks swirled. Lights glistened. No one seemed aware of their intimate *tête-à-tête* amidst the corner holly bushes and jeweler's cotton that was meant to be snow.

"I do not dare become more familiar with you, my lord," she confessed, using her most scolding tone. "You have done enough irreparable damage to my reputation for one day."

"I am the man who will be your husband, Alexandra," he said simply, shocking her with his pronouncement. "Would you not care to get to know me?"

His words chilled her. She stepped to the side, slipping from his warm presence and putting a more respectable distance between them. "My brother has spoken to you, then, and that is the reason for our discourse this evening."

"I have spoken with your brother, yes." He matched her steps, effectively boxing her in against the holly once more. His jaw tightened as his gaze swept her face. "But he did not give me permission to ask for your hand. Thus, in answer to your question, no, my dialogue with Ravenscroft is not the reason I'm standing before you."

She wanted to believe him. Her foolish, foolish heart fluttered. Hope, a chimera she had long believed buried, flitted to the surface. Could this witty, beautiful man truly want her for herself and not because he had lost his head and ruined her in the carriage before witnesses?

"What is the reason?" she dared to ask.

"Is it not apparent, Danvers?" His grin returned in full force, and Lord Harry Marlow at his most charming was a magnificent sight to behold, even for a practical woman of science such as herself.

If her heart beat faster and heat slid through her body like warm honey, it could not be helped. As objective as she liked to believe herself, before her—and within her flustered reaction—stood the proof that she was only human, all too susceptible to a rakish smile and a knowing touch. And lips that knew how to coax and fingers that knew just how to pluck her hungry nipples…

No. She must not allow herself to stray once more into ruin.

She took a deep breath and recalled the conversation. "Nothing is apparent, Lord Harry. Surely you ought to know that the world is never what it seems."

"All too true," he acknowledged with a grim air that suggested he felt the meaning of those words to his core. "But the reason I'm standing before you now is that I want you to be my wife. I want to kiss you and touch you the way I did in the carriage earlier today, only I do not want to stop until we have both reached our pinnacles. First, however, I want to dance with you."

Shocked by his admission, Alexandra allowed him to take

her hand and tuck it into his elbow. Allowed him also to steer her into the heavy sea of revelers. Allowed him to sweep her into a waltz and plant unwanted notions inside her mind.

"What do you mean by 'pinnacles'?" she asked as he guided her round the floor as if she were the keenest dancer he had ever partnered with.

Lord Harry gave a laugh, keeping his gaze trained high above her head. She watched, mesmerized, as his prominent Adam's apple dipped in his strong throat, the only indication that her query had affected him.

"Give me time, Danvers, and you shall see," he promised.

Chapter Six

>>>><<<<

𝓑OSWELL HOUSE WAS a monstrosity, it was true. Even with one hundred seventy-six chambers amongst its sprawling wings, there was not one room that called to Harry the way its lake did. The lake was vast, settled into the land naturally so Boswell House presided over it like a monarch reigning upon a throne. As lads, Harry and Spencer had fished in the lake, had splashed in it, had paddled about in wooden boats pretending to be invading navies.

It seemed somehow fitting to return to the lake now with snow a pristine white along its banks and ice forming a beautiful, silver crust of skin over the waters. Especially with Lady Alexandra at his side.

"How lovely," she exclaimed softly, taking in the view of the glistening wintry lake.

The crisp cold of the air kissed her cheeks with a becoming blossom of pink, and her blue eyes were wide. A stray tendril of copper hair had worked its way free of her coiffure and blew across her freckled nose.

"The loveliest," he agreed, unable to resist catching the flyaway curl and tucking it behind her ear.

This woman was going to be his wife. How impossible it seemed that days ago, she had not been a part of his life when now he could not fathom a future without her in it. Looking at her took his breath and made his chest feel at once light as a

THE NIGHT BEFORE SCANDAL

bird and heavy as a boulder. It was the strangest sensation, defying description, and he had never experienced anything comparable.

"You are not even looking at the lake, my lord," she pointed out softly, the color in her cheeks deepening beneath his regard.

"No," he agreed, unable to look away from her. "I am not."

"Cease tarrying, brother," called Spencer then, interrupting the moment. "By the time you finish gazing into Lady Alexandra's eyes, it shall be the spring thaw and all the ice will have melted."

"Rotter," he muttered beneath his breath, for his brother was no better. He was lovesick for his wife. Louder, he called, "We merely stopped to enjoy the view."

"I heard that, and I am not a rotter," Spencer returned amiably. "I have excellent ears, you realize."

"For an old man," Harry quipped. In truth, Spencer was only a few years his senior, but that did not mean he was above making the jab, particularly when his brother was enjoying his discomfit so damned much.

"I distinctly recall sharing a boyhood with you, so if I am an old man, I am afraid you are as well," Spencer said, quirking a brow.

"You always made me be the Spanish Armada," he remembered without heat. "And then you insisted upon defeating me."

"I wanted to be Sir Francis Drake," his brother admitted, grinning unrepentantly. "We could not both be England, after all. There can be one victor and one loser, dear brother."

As the heir, Spencer had always gotten what he wanted. The trend had not ended when they had become men. Boadicea was the personification of that fact, but somehow, with Lady Alexandra clinging to his arm, Harry no longer felt the ache of remorse or the stinging sense of loss he had once felt whenever he considered the woman his brother had taken as his bride. There was instead a sense of rightness settling over him, the knowledge that though he had not been able to see it at the time, something—or rather *someone*—more uniquely suited to him had come along.

And he could be happy with that someone. Happier than he could have been with any other woman. He knew this instinctively, and the more he considered what Spencer had said to him, the more he knew his brother was right. He could have lost his head with any number of ladies over the years, and yet it had only been her.

Lady Alexandra Danvers.

"While I would dearly love to listen to the two of you argue about playing naval heroes in your youth, the day is cold, and I fear I shall not last much longer outdoors," interrupted Boadicea then. "We have not even skated yet."

The feelings he had once nurtured for her had altered, and thank God for that. He could not spend the rest of his days mooning after his brother's wife, regardless of how lovely and witty she was.

"I have never skated before," Lady Alexandra ventured then. "I must admit that balancing one's self upon sharp blades atop a layer of ice covering a large body of water seems like a rather poor choice to make. A form of torture, perhaps, rather than an entertainment."

Harry chuckled. The intricacies and eccentricities of her mind would never cease intriguing him, he was certain of it. "When you phrase it in such a fashion, the art does sound questionable indeed."

She flashed him a smile he felt in his gut. "The art of madmen, one might say."

"You only say so because you have never skated before, my lady," Spencer said.

What a happy little quartet they made, just the four of them and a handful of servants, having left the rest of the revelers behind in the warmth of Boswell House. Snowflakes began to gently drift from the sky in that moment, flitting to earth like tiny bits of down. Harry could not have imagined such a day, when he could peacefully coexist with Spencer and Boadicea and not have the splinter of jealousy embedded painfully within him.

"You shall have Lord Harry to hold on to if you lose your balance," Boadicea told Lady Alexandra, her eyes twinkling. "Surely that is the antidote to the torture."

Lady Alexandra flushed adorably once more. "There is that to recommend it, I suppose."

She supposed? How he wanted to kiss the coyness from her lips. Instead, he covered her hand on his arm with his, giving her fingers a gentle squeeze. "Careful now or you shall bruise my pride unalterably, my dear."

Her lush mouth twitched, her eyes gleaming with mirth into his. There in that moment, snow swirling around them, laughter in his heart and on her lips, he felt the slide begin. The inevitable, inexorable pull to this woman above all others. He could not shake the belief she was the other half to make him whole. The woman who would drive him to distraction, now and forever.

"You shall have to prove it to me, my lord." She gave him a minx's smile, and he could not deny he was smitten.

He would do his damnedest for the rest of their lives to prove it to her, if she would but let him. "I am ever a man who appreciates a challenge."

"Come," Spencer said then, an unwelcome interruption. "The servants have laid out benches for us to put on our ice skates."

For a moment, Harry had forgotten he and Lady Alexandra were not alone. It was a jarring realization. But he guided her to the benches just the same. In no time, the four of them had donned their skates and had made their trek to the lake's frozen surface.

Spencer and Boadicea wasted no time, skating onto the ice hand in hand. With a sound of undeniable, almost childlike joy, Boadicea skated in a circle about Spencer, arms wide, beaming at him. Lady Alexandra remained rooted to the shore, however, her fingers digging into Harry's arm.

He turned to her. "Do you not wish to skate, my lady?"

"It is not skating itself I fear," she admitted softly, "but falling."

"I cannot help but to think that a most rational and normal fear." Her errant curl was back, and he once more stowed it behind her ear, allowing his gloved fingers to linger there. "But if you do not try, you will never master the art. And if you do not master the art, you will be bound to fall again and again."

She wrinkled her nose. "Or I can simply avoid ice-covered lakes for the rest of my life."

"Also a rational decision," he agreed, studying her face, memorizing the contours, the shape of her freckles, the fullness of her lips. God, she was gorgeous, and interesting and so bloody smart. "Except, if you avoid ice-covered lakes, you will also forever be denied the delight of sliding across them on sharp blades."

"Who invented such a ludicrous notion, do you suppose?" she asked, smiling at him yet again.

"Someone who lived near a frozen lake and spent the winter gazing upon its icy expanse, thinking traversing it sounded like great fun," he suggested.

She pursed her lips. "Is it great fun? It seems to me the inventor was far more likely to have been someone who needed to cross the frozen lake for survival rather than entertainment."

Of course his science-minded lady would think so.

"Come with me and discover the answer for yourself," he invited, guiding her toward the edge.

Spencer and Boadicea had skated a good distance away, beyond earshot but well within sight. It was just as well, for though Harry enjoyed having Lady Alexandra alone, he could not control himself. Here, he could speak freely and yet be forced to refrain from further compromising her.

"I do not know," she said then, the hesitancy in her voice giving him pause. "Perhaps you ought to skate without me, my lord."

Where was the bold, daring creature who strutted about in her brother's trousers and boots?

"Do you trust me, Danvers?" he asked her sternly, tipping up her chin and holding it in a gentle touch, forcing her to meet his gaze.

Her brilliant eyes scorched him alive. Copper lashes fluttered over them, hiding them for a moment as she searched inside herself for the answer. He waited, holding his breath, his body tensing. If she said no…

"Yes," she said, giving him another beautiful, soft smile. "I do, Lord Harry."

Victory flared within him, and her words made his chest swell. Absurdly, he wanted to shout out the announcement, hear it echo in the hushed stillness of the winter world.

But he did not. Instead, he slowly led her onto the ice. When her skates first made contact with the lake's frozen skin, she wobbled, clutching at him frantically, her eyes wide with alarm.

"Oh, Lord Harry," she protested. "Perhaps this is a bad idea. Perhaps we ought to merely sit beneath the warm furs back on the benches while the duke and duchess skate. We could have a delightful conversation and sip mulled wine instead of falling on our rumps and breaking our limbs."

He shook his head slowly, his gaze hovering over her lips of their own accord. How he longed to feel it beneath his once more, so soft and smooth and supple and delicious. "This is a far better idea, for it means I can once more have my arms around you."

"Oh," she said again, sounding breathless. "Yes. There is that to commend skating, after all. Likely the only thing, I fear. Have you not wondered what would happen if the ice should break?"

There went her mind again.

"No. The lake here is not overly deep, and there are plenty of able-bodied men about to assist us should we require it."

"But my lord—"

"Hush." He skated backward, pulling her with him, and after a glance over his shoulder toward Spencer and Boadicea, then another for the servants on the bank to make certain no one was paying them any heed, he acted, pressing his lips over hers, firm and swift. The contact was hot, the connection between them just as passionate and overwhelming as it had been in the carriage.

Before he could be tempted to deepen the kiss, he pulled away, smiling down into her dazed expression. "There is also *that* to commend skating."

"I think you are persuading me the art of ice skating may not be solely reserved for madmen after all," she said, staring at his lips as the snowflakes danced around them.

Another surreptitious glance revealed everyone else was still distracted. "Are you entirely persuaded, my lady?"

Catching on to his game, she shook her head in the negative, her countenance grave. "I do believe I require some additional persuasion, Lord Harry. If you are able to offer some, that is."

He skated them in a circle, kissing her soundly as he did so, this time allowing his tongue to trace the seam of her lips and then sink inside for a taste before lifting his mouth from hers. "How about now?"

"Hmm." She pretended to contemplate. "Perhaps just a bit more."

Laughing with unrestrained joy, he kissed her yet again. Kissed her harder, open-mouthed and hungry, forgetting where they were, forgetting they possessed an audience, forgetting he was meant to act with propriety. Until the sound of skates carving the ice pierced the fog of desire clouding his brain.

He broke away from Lady Alexandra as Spencer and Boadicea skated toward them.

"Try to conduct yourself with a regard for the proprieties, brother," Spencer cautioned, every bit the icy duke with his reproach before he winked, softening the grim starch of his countenance. "I would hate to see Ravenscroft break your nose as he threatened. The Marlow family nose is perfectly straight, you know, Lady Alexandra. I daresay you would not like Harry's pretty face to become so afflicted, would you?"

Boadicea gave Spencer a playful swat. "Do behave, husband."

"Me?" he asked with mock innocence. "Behave? Wherever did you get such a ludicrous notion?"

Their love for each other was as nauseating as ever. But this time, it did not nettle him. Did not burrow beneath his skin or chafe him. This time, he held a woman in his arms who was warm and lovely and sweet-scented.

"Julian did not dare to threaten your nose, did he?" Lady Alexandra demanded, searching Harry's gaze.

"Not in so many words, my dear," he soothed, shooting his brother a venomous look of stern reproach. One day, he would get even with the blighter. One day. "If you will excuse us, I am doing my utmost to teach Lady Alexandra how to ice skate."

Slowly, he guided her across the frozen lake, putting some distance between them and his laughing brother, who was once again enjoying himself far too much. As Harry watched, Spencer whispered something into Boadicea's ear, and she threw back her head for a delighted laugh.

He turned his attention to the woman in his arms as he held her tightly round the waist and led her farther away. A snowflake stuck to her lashes, then another to her lips before melting. She was stunning, like some sort of pagan ice goddess come to life. And she was his. All his.

"You need not fear for my nose," he told her at last with a smile. "I have every intention of winning you over."

She gazed up at him as if she were seeing him, truly seeing him for the first time. "I am beginning to fear you already have, my lord."

He could not quell the raging rush of desire and happiness that assailed him at her words. How grateful he was he had taken her skating, for what better excuse to hold her in his arms?

He suppressed the urge to kiss her again, tamping it ruthlessly down. "Good. That is precisely what I wish to hear."

The day was bright all around them, filled with the brilliance of the sun reflecting off all that pure snow. Flurries continued to dance from the sky in intervals. They skated for hours, hand in hand, until their cheeks were flushed, until they were laughing, until they had stolen at least half a dozen more kisses from each other when heads were turned.

The ice did not crack, and neither did anyone break a limb, though Lady Alexandra did fall on her rump once, much to her chagrin. Afterward, they shared warm mulled wine and sat beneath furs, watching the snow as it began to fall in earnest. The sensation in Harry's chest blossomed and swelled.

It had a name: happiness.

And it had a source: Lady Alexandra Danvers.

Chapter Seven

→→→»«←←←

*L*ORD HARRY MARLOW possessed more charm than a human male ought to be physically capable of producing. So much charm it seemed to defy the laws of science. As Alexandra roamed the extensive gardens of Boswell Manor on her own, boots crunching through the snow, she decided he must be an oddity. An outlier. For not only was he beautiful, and not only did his kisses make her weak, and not only was he capable of setting her at ease in a way no other suitor had, but he was also achingly kind and clever.

Over the course of the house party, he had been attentive, making every effort to spend time in her presence. Through all the entertainments planned, from trimming the tree to caroling to Christmas charades, he had not strayed far from her side. When he was not in a chamber, it seemed less gay for his absence, and she found herself waiting restlessly for his appearance.

To say her reaction to him was vexing was an understatement. The strange, quivery feelings he produced within her with nothing more than his presence baffled her. It was as if her body was attuned to him, as if some deep, primal part of her recognized its mate.

She did not like it.

He was a beautiful distraction, keeping her from the pursuit of far more worthy causes than stolen kisses and silken touches beneath her skirts. Why, she had not even added to her weather prognostics map in all the time since their infamous carriage ride together. Her head needed to take the reins from her heart, and she had to stop this silly longing for the man.

For though he was endlessly charming, she could not shake the needling suspicion he acted out of a sense of duty. The Duke of Bainbridge's teasing words from their skating party returned to her. *I would hate to see Ravenscroft break your nose as he threatened.*

Was he only being charming because of the threat Julian had made against him? Or because of the threat of scandal that would taint him and his reputation if they did not wed?

He was an MP, after all, and he needed to maintain his good standing. A sudden gust of wind sent snow into her face from the hedges she meandered between. It was as if mother nature had sneezed upon her. She stopped, blinking to clear the snow from her lashes and dab at her nose.

"Allow me."

The voice, butter smooth and rich and deep, sent the same ripple of warmth through her it always did. She blinked some more, and there he was, the object of her frustrated musings, as golden and gorgeous as a god in the winter's sun. Her heart pumped frantically as he gently dabbed at her face with a monogrammed handkerchief that smelled deliciously of him.

"Thank you, my lord," she said softly, willing herself to become inured to his allure.

She held still for his ministrations, telling herself she must end this fascination she had for him. She must be stern and strong. She must cleave to science, to her principles. She had never intended to marry, and there was no reason to change her mind now.

No reason at all.

Except...

"You are the loveliest creature I have ever seen, like a snow fairy queen here in the midst of all this winter's white." His gloves fingers brushed her chin, tipping it up. "May I kiss you, Lady Alexandra?"

If he kissed her, he would erase her ability to think. All logic would flee from her mind, disappearing like the sun from the sky before a sudden summer storm.

Her lips parted. She was going to tell him no, but then she made the mistake of falling into his eyes.

"Yes," she breathed. "Please do."

And then his mouth was upon hers, firm and warm and knowing, at once familiar and new. Thrilling. Delicious. Everything she wanted without knowing she needed it. She forgot all her earlier determination, abandoned it to the wind as if it had never been.

For how could she think of anything but Lord Harry when his lips were coaxing hers in the sweetest possible way?

Her hands found his shoulders, then twined around his neck, and she pressed herself shamelessly against him, her breasts crushed to the broad strength of his chest, her skirts trapped between their seeking limbs. The brims of their hats knocked together, and hers gave way, falling down her back to land in the snow.

She didn't care what happened to the hat.

She didn't care about keeping him at bay.

All she cared about was his kiss.

Thank heavens they were alone in the gardens and obstructed from the view of the main house by the immaculately manicured hedges. More scandal was the last thing either of them needed.

She parted for him on a sigh of pure need, and his tongue

slipped inside her mouth. He tasted of tea and sugar and himself, that dark and divine temptation she had come to know as *Harry*. He groaned as if he was as tortured as she felt, everything inside her clamoring for more, for more than she could comprehend.

The kiss deepened, and then she knocked his hat from his head too, and her fingers were somehow in his hair, and she was shamelessly arching into him, sucking on his tongue. That was the problem with Lord Harry Marlow—he was intoxicating, and whenever she was in his presence or in his arms, he consumed her every thought.

He was all she wanted.

Could she not have him and her intellectual pursuits? Could not a woman of science also have…whatever *this* was?

The greediness within her told her she could. If it was real, what he felt for her—and it certainly felt real now, as real as that part of his anatomy which was currently prodding her—she could become his wife without losing anything. Indeed, for the first time, it occurred to her all she would gain in marrying Lord Harry.

Him and all his glorious kisses and wicked touches and sinful embraces.

Oh.

He dragged his mouth down her throat, sucking her sensitized flesh, and she tipped her head back, granting him access above the collar of her coat. It may have been a frigid winter's day, but she was aflame, burning from the inside out, and not even her toes were cold in her boots. He warmed her in a way the sun could not, from deep within, in that secret place she had never before realized existed.

But just as quickly as his kisses had begun, so too did they end. He withdrew his mouth, staring down at her with eyes that blazed with verdant fire. If gazes could consume, he swallowed her whole now, and she was a willing sacrifice.

"I could kiss you all day and never stop," he said gruffly, passing his gloved thumb over her lower lip once, then twice. "But I fear if I carry on in this fashion, I shall have your skirts up around your waist, and I shall be on my knees before you in the snow, and that is the sort of scandal neither of us can weather."

She struggled to catch her breath, for her wits to return. The world around her seemed somehow different after that kiss, the greenery even brighter as it peeked from beneath white caps of snow, the sky overhead impossibly blue, more brilliant than she had ever seen it before, not a cloud as far as she could see.

"Not to mention," she forced herself to say, striving to be flippant, as if he had not just changed everything, "the damage the snow would do to your trousers. And I daresay kneeling in the snow would prove dreadfully cold. Your kneecaps might freeze."

What a stupid thing to say, and she wished she could recall it the moment it left her tongue. But it was too late. His regard did not change, however. He continued to watch her as if he wanted to devour her. And she liked it.

"I would gladly kneel before you in the snow any day, Danvers, frozen kneecaps or no." His lips quirked up in a slow smile, and there, once more, was his effortless, abundant charm.

Her stomach quivered. "First your nose and now your knees. It would seem the Danvers family has nefarious designs upon your person."

She had not meant to reference Julian's threats, but they were once more foremost in her mind, mingling with the fear the man before her did not truly want her. Alexandra's pride would not allow her to be the woman any man was forced to wed.

He grimaced. "Pray forgive my brother's ill attempt at humor. I fear it is not a talent at which he excels."

She did not doubt Bainbridge's words had been spoken partially in jest, but she also knew her brother, and Julian was fiercely protective of the women in his life. He had likely delivered some manner of threat, and if there was ever a time to work out once and for all, whether Lord Harry was being pressured to court her, it was now.

"I am certain Julian was a beast," she said. "He is as protective as a mama bear. But I need you to know that I do not want to be a duty, not to you or any other man. I would far rather be a desire."

He cupped her face then, with such a ginger, reverent touch she could have sighed again. "You are anything but a duty. I desire you more than I have ever desired another."

Her breath caught, and she searched his eyes, uncertain if she dared believe him. "You do?"

"I do," he affirmed without pause. "More than any other."

More than Boadicea? The unworthy thought leapt to her mind, but she dismissed it. His kisses in the carriage and on every occasion since had dispelled the rumor that he was in love with the Duchess of Bainbridge.

"You have not been courting me because you have no choice?" she persisted.

He was so handsome, the sun making his blond hair glint as if it were made of pure gold, that he stole her breath. His smile deepened, creating small crinkles at the corners of his eyes that she found endlessly riveting.

What would he do, she wondered, if she kissed him there? And why did that small imperfection on his otherwise flawless face affect her so? Why did it make her long for him even more?

"My dear Danvers, I have been courting you because I wish to make you my wife. And because now I have had a trousers wearing weather prognosticator in my arms, I cannot fathom ever settling for anyone else."

His words should not have settled in her heart like a promise, but they did.

And she should not have reached for him once more, drawing his mouth down to hers for another kiss, but she did.

This kiss felt different. It felt like the beginning.

She stepped back before either of them could deepen the kiss, her lips tingling. "I had better get back to the party before I am missed. We must think of your poor kneecaps, after all."

He threw back his head and laughed, and the sound echoed through the quiet of the garden, laden with the same promise and joy she felt bursting to life within her.

Chapter Eight

"I AM SO happy to have caught you alone."

Harry, poring over a book in his brother's private library and nursing a brandy, started at the sound of his sister-in-law's voice. Boadicea sailed over the threshold in that boisterous yet elegant way she had, resplendent in her aubergine afternoon gown, her distinctive auburn hair swept into a Grecian braid. A pleasant warmth infused his chest at the sight of her, just as it would with any cherished acquaintance he was pleased to see.

He stood, acknowledging her presence. "What do you require of me, sister dear?"

Yes, it still smarted a bit to call her *sister*, but he knew the source of that emotion all too well: his pride. Spencer had won her heart, and as much as Harry loved his brother, losing to him in the battle for a lady's hand nevertheless stung. He had always been the charming brother. He ought to have won.

And yet, looking upon her now, glowing with happiness, and beset by a new, previously unimaginable fascination for Lady Alexandra Danvers, he could not help but be relieved that he had not.

Boadicea stopped when she reached him, her blue eyes bright with excitement. "What do you think of Lady Alexandra?"

Bloody hell. She had sought him out on a matchmaking

expedition. The truth of it was, he had spent the last week courting the lady in question by any means possible. He skated with her on Boswell Manor's frozen pond—she had fallen on her rump and blushed so red her cheeks had put apples to shame. He danced with her, sang carols with her, took her for a walk in the gardens after the snow finally ended. He chatted with her. He wondered if her allure would ever lessen. Somehow, it only increased with each day.

But that did not mean he wished to examine the way he felt for Lady Alexandra with Boadicea now. Or ever.

He raised a brow. "I think I have compromised her and am obligated to marry her."

She tapped him on the arm. "But do you like her? Are you in love with her?"

"Of course I like her," he was quick to admit. Perhaps too quick. "She is intelligent and unique, and her wit never ceases to entertain me. She is also beautiful."

And about as graceful as a plow horse, but he found her lack of affectation endearing. She was unapologetically herself, and damn if it didn't make him want her all the more.

"Are you in love with her?" Boadicea persisted, slanting him a knowing look. "I have been watching the two of you together all week, and Spencer thinks me quite silly, but you are such a well-matched pair. Lady Alexandra is a member of my Lady's Suffrage Society, you know, and she is not only clever but kindhearted and good. She is exactly the sort of wife you deserve."

After one week, he was not prepared to say he was in love. The last time he'd imagined himself embroiled in that finer emotion, he had been hopelessly wrong. He did not dare trust himself now. Did he?

"I like her," he allowed. "Do not meddle, Boadicea."

"Meddle?" She pressed a hand to her heart and sent him a

look of feigned innocence. "Why would you ever think me capable of such a thing?"

He tamped down the grin that threatened to give him away. "Because I know you."

"I may have provided Lady Alexandra with some guidance," his sister-in-law confessed without a hint of contrition. "But before I tell you anything more, I must be reassured that your intentions are honorable. Look me in the eye and promise me, Harry Archibald Marlow."

Good God, she had invoked his hated full name. He had revealed it to her just the once, and the minx had never forgotten. But part of him was clamoring to know what sort of guidance Boadicea could have given Lady Alexandra, and what it meant for him. The wickedness within him dared hope it involved some time away from the watchful eyes of their friends and family and fellow revelers, who were attuned to the slightest impropriety.

"You must never call me that," he gritted. "But you have my promise that my intentions toward Lady Alexandra are only honorable. I mean to make her my wife. Now please do elaborate upon the aforementioned *guidance* you gave my future betrothed."

Boadicea winked. "Oh, I shan't tell you a thing! That would spoil the surprise. But if I were you, I would find the nearest opportunity to find my way to the north tower."

The north tower was precisely where he had intended to take Lady Alexandra that first day before the rude interruption of their families and fellow guests. "The north tower? You do realize that it has not been habitable since my grandfather was a lad, do you not?"

It was an exaggeration, but not much of one. The north tower was part of the original castle that Boswell House had been built around, and it was drafty and dark and filled with the ghosts of the past.

"Perhaps it is not as unwelcoming as you think," Boadicea said. "Go have a look for yourself, Harry."

His mind was instantly inundated with an image of Lady Alexandra—Danvers, as he liked to think of her—alone in the north tower, conducting meteorological studies, her fingers smudged with ink as she fretted over her prognostics map.

"Perhaps I will," he said with casual nonchalance, as though the mere thought of Danvers with her odd little tool and her enthusiasm for the scientific didn't make his cock go half-rigid in his trousers.

"Oh you will." Her smile was knowing. "Promise me once more, Harry Archibald Marlow."

"I promise you that I will make Lady Alexandra my wife if she and her irate brother will have me," he grumbled. "I also promise you that further use of my middle name will result in me watering your holly bushes in a fashion you will not appreciate."

Yes, he would piss in her potted holly. Why not? He was feeling rather reckless these days, and he had nothing left to lose.

Her mouth formed a perfect O of astonishment. "Harry Arch—"

"Do you dare to risk it?" he interrupted, pleased with himself for shocking her. Boadicea was not easily surprised.

She pressed her lips together. "No. Be gone with you. But be forewarned that I may have shared your full name with Lady Alexandra."

He ground his teeth as he left the library to the sound of his sister-in-law's laughter. If Danvers invoked his hated full name, he had a different sort of punishment in mind for her. And it would be far more pleasurable than relieving himself in his sister-in-law's living Christmas decorations.

THE NORTH TOWER of Boswell House was like an enchanted world. Alexandra could not have been more pleased that Boadicea had shown her this room, so far away from the main house and all its occupants. It was the proper height for meteorological observance. But even with its fresh new paint, sumptuous carpets, and comfortable furniture—not to mention the sunlight that filtered in the windows—to delight, studying the weather was not her primary pursuit.

Instead, she was sitting, legs tucked beneath her, draped on a particularly comfortable divan, flipping through the pages of a book that was riveting, shocking, and intriguing all at once. Boadicea had given her the thin, leather-bound volume, requiring her complete discretion.

It was an illegal book, filled with naughtiness. With lewdness and lasciviousness.

Naturally, Alexandra had given her promise to keep the book's existence to herself.

She was curious, after all. Horridly, thoroughly curious.

Lord Harry had awakened a wickedness inside her that had been slumbering but was now decidedly awake. The wickedness was restless. It wanted more. The pages she'd turned thus far had certainly aided in that mission.

Naughty grooms.

Wicked maids.

Tongues that performed improper feats upon unmentionable places.

Her cheeks were hot, the flesh between her thighs tingling with anticipation as she turned each page. And she could not stop reading. She forgot about her intentions to measure the temperature and sky for her map. She forgot about everything and everyone in these stolen, quiet moments to herself.

Everyone but Lord Harry, that was.

For he never seemed to stray far from her thoughts.

"What are you reading?"

Alexandra yelped, the forbidden book she'd been devouring nearly leaping from her hands in her discomfit. She turned to the source of that delicious voice to find that Lord Harry had appeared as if conjured from her fantasies.

Except he was more sinfully handsome than her woeful imagination could recall. Though he had not strayed far from her side for the last sennight, each time she saw him, her body gave an instinctive, inward sigh of appreciation.

He stole her breath. Her gaze traveled hungrily over his golden hair, high forehead, the blade of his nose, high cheekbones, that firm, rugged jaw. He was tall and broad and muscled.

And he was staring at her in an intent, expectant fashion.

Belatedly, she forced herself to stop ogling him and respond to his query. "Something quite edifying." She snapped the book shut and stuffed it beneath her skirt. "What are you doing here, Lord Harry?"

"Edifying," he repeated, sauntering toward her as though the two of them alone in a far-off tower was the most natural and inevitable thing in the world. "What is the subject?"

Alexandra watched helplessly as he skirted the divan and settled himself next to her, his strong horseman's thighs splaying wide enough to touch hers. She swallowed, took a breath, and dismissed any inconvenient thoughts or emotions that would have impeded her ability to behave.

Or so she thought. The leather cover of the book, trapped between her skirt-clad thigh and the cushion, seemed to burn her fingers.

She blinked, focused on Lord Harry. "The subjects are varied. It is a collection of short stories."

"What manner of stories?"

Alexandra forced herself to frown at him, ignoring his question. "Surely you must realize better than anyone that your presence here, with me, is unacceptable. We have already created the scandal of the year together, and I shudder to think what will happen if you are found alone with me."

A lone, golden brow raised. "You do realize, do you not Danvers, that the year is nearly over? As such, we can create as much scandal as possible, given that it will cancel itself out upon the new year. Further, no one will find us here together. We are well beyond the reach of other guests. Indeed, we could safely remain here for the next day and no one would be the wiser."

His words warmed parts of her she had not previously known existed. "Your logic is regrettably unsound, Lord Harry. The end of one year and the beginning of another has no bearing upon a scandal. A mark upon one's character cannot be removed by the mere changing of a number."

His expression sobered, his eyes intense as they bored into hers. "You are right, my lady. It cannot. But it can be ameliorated by actions taken to rectify the mistake."

She stiffened, diverting her gaze from him. "Am I a mistake to you, my lord?"

Lord, she hated to think that was how he viewed her. That she was one of his regrets. That he wished he had never kissed her in the carriage. She did not want to be a burden to anyone. Nor did she desire for Lord Harry to sacrifice himself for her upon the matrimonial altar.

"No." His fingers brushed over her jaw gently, turning her face back to his. The decadent green of his eyes took her breath as she fell into them. "You could never be a mistake to me. But my disregard for your virtue was. And now you will be forced to pay the forfeit for my massive error in judgment."

His words failed to mollify her. He had already told her he intended to marry her that night at the Welcome Ball, and he had courted her with steadfast attention in the week since, but she would not be his burden. She had been adamant that she would not wed. Regardless of the damage to her reputation, she did not need to marry Lord Harry. When Julian had married a wealthy American heiress, he had settled a handsome sum upon her as dowry. She was reasonably certain that her brother could be persuaded to enable her to access the funds.

She did not move from Lord Harry's touch, for she relished his nearness and the slow stroke of his caress on her skin. But neither did she hesitate to tell him the truth of the matter. "Lord Harry, I will not be forced into anything, least of all nuptials."

A frown marred his forehead, but even in his displeasure, he was so handsome he made her ache. "Do you not wish to marry me, my lady?"

"You have not yet proposed," she pointed out. "Thus far, you have expressed a desire to make me your wife, but you have also spoken of mistakes and scandal and errors. If you feel obligated to ask for my hand because of what happened in the carriage, allow me to relieve you of that worry. My brother is prepared to settle a handsome amount upon me, and I do not need to marry you to obtain it."

He blinked, the corners of his supple mouth turning down all the more. That elegant brow of his furrowed. "I beg your pardon, my lady. Are you suggesting that you wed another man in my stead?"

She pursed her lips, considering the suggestion objectively. "I am certain I could find any number of suitors who are pockets to let and only all too eager for the opportunity to fill their coffers with my sister-in-law's American gold. Of course, there is always the other, far more preferable option that I simply remain unwed and collect the funds myself so that I may live my life as I wish, dedicated to the pursuit of science."

His hand had traveled to the side of her face, cupping it tenderly, his thumb stroking over her ear. She had never found the ear to be a receptive or particularly delightful appendage—aside from the mechanical necessity of hearing, naturally—but ever since Lord Harry had appeared in her life, she was heartily rethinking her dismissal of it and any number of other body parts.

The pad of his thumb stroking over her ear's delicate shell was enough to make a sharp pang of need surge through her.

"Alexandra."

Her name in his dark, sensual voice caught her attention. A frisson of something delightfully wicked licked down her spine. She stared at his lips, noting how finely formed they were for what had to be the fiftieth time. "Yes?"

"Do you wish to marry another? Is there some other gentleman who has claimed your affections?" His voice was strained as he posed the curt questions.

"Of course not." She blinked. "If I must marry any man, I would choose you, my lord. Supposing you had asked for my hand, of course. Which you have decidedly not, thus far."

His thumb stroked from her ear to her cheekbone, gliding in such a tantalizing caress that she shivered. "You do not inspire a great deal of confidence in a man. Should I ask, what would your answer be, my lady? I have half a notion to expect you to tell me to turn around and never look back."

Somehow, the thought of Lord Harry Marlow leaving her made her mouth go dry. It was lunacy, for she had only known him for little more than a week's time. But already, she knew the heat of his lips on hers, his hands roaming her body, the taste of him, his heartbeat's rapid thrum.

"Forgive me, my lord." She paused, gathering her thoughts, for this was one area of her life that never failed to cause her any number of difficulties. "There is no one else. I merely relish my liberty, and I imagine you do the same. Do you wish to ask for my hand? To truly ask? Not out of duty or necessity but out of want?"

"I want you, yes."

"To marry me," she pressed. "Wanting to marry me is a different beast entirely from merely desiring me physically, my lord."

"Agreed." He paused, his touch remaining upon her in a way she liked far, far too much. "This thing between us is sudden, I know. Perhaps it is the spirit of the Christmas season, or perhaps I have taken leave of my senses, but the moment I saw you standing in the snow, I knew I had to make you mine."

He had? She frowned. "But you thought I was a gentleman."

"No." He shook his head, a slow, sensual grin curving his lips. "I always knew you were a female."

The scoundrel. Had he been having her on? She wouldn't have thought it in him, for though his kisses and caresses were most wicked, his reputation was above reproach. "You called me Mr. Danvers."

He pressed his lips together, attempting to squelch his smirk and failing. His fingers followed the line of her throat in a gentle sweep that made her ache. "I wanted to nettle you, I'm afraid. You were being frightfully highhanded for a lady dressed in her brother's ill-fitting clothing, standing about in the snow. I wanted to rattle you a bit, but I also wanted to get you alone so that I could kiss you."

Oh my.

Warmth suffused the region of her heart. Her stomach performed an odd little somersault. My God, he was charming. And infectious. The urge to spend the rest of her days thus hit her: staring into his emerald gaze, kissing those splendidly formed lips, and chatting with him in such a cozy fashion that the scent and warmth of him washed over her like a golden glow.

"You are quite the rogue, my lord," she observed, willing her restless heart to calm itself. She could not be falling in love with Lord Harry Marlow after knowing him for all of a week. Could she? As a woman of science, she could not credit it. And yet, the evidence was there in her wild pulse, the tingling settling between her thighs, the hunger roaring through her.

"A rogue who very much wishes to marry you, my lady. If you will have me." His hand splayed over her heart, bare skin upon bare skin, absorbing the frantic beats. "Will you have me?"

She blessed fashion for the cut of her ribbon-trimmed décolletage. The rational part of her, the science-minded part of her that believed in observation, in facts and reason, knew then what she must do. It would be a bold move, perhaps foolhardy, and certainly hazardous for her already tarnished reputation.

But it was the only move she could fathom. It was the sole manner by which she would be able to determine whether or not they were truly compatible, and whether the feelings he inspired in her were physical or had their roots in something more.

The book she'd been reading gave her the boldness she required. Was this not a new era, and was she not an independent-minded female capable of making her own decisions and forging her way in the world?

Yes. It was. She was.

Alexandra took a deep, fortifying breath. "I will marry you on one condition, Lord Harry. You must first engage in sexual congress with me."

Chapter Nine

>>>><<<<

*H*ARRY STARED AT Lady Alexandra Danvers.
She did not look mad.
Neither did she appear soused.

Which thoroughly dispelled the only two explanations for what he had just heard her say. Unless…he supposed it possible. His great-uncle Xavier had been as deaf as a snuff box. Surely he was beginning to lose his sense of hearing at an inordinately early age.

Either that, or the gorgeous, eccentric, lush woman before him had just invited him to bed her. Without benefit of marriage. Good God.

Perhaps he was not her first lover. There was yet another solid explanation for the words that had just fallen from her pink, soft lips. Lips he suddenly envisioned circling his cock. If she was not an innocent, that certainly changed matters. He couldn't lie. The possibilities such a thing brought to mind were as delightful as they were depraved.

The breath hissed from his lungs as the erection of the century sprang to rigid life in his trousers. Damnation. What could he do?

"I beg your pardon," he said with great difficulty, for all the blood in his body seemed to have rushed to his groin. "What did you just say, my lady?"

Lady Alexandra held his gaze. Blue, copper-lash-studded

eyes stared into his, unblinking. "I said that I will marry you if you bed me. I should have added one caveat, however. I consider this to be a scientific experiment, you see. If you bed me, and I am provided with ample proof that we are compatible, I will wed you."

Holy hell. Of its own accord, his hand slid lower until the lush, heavy weight of her corseted breast filled it. He could not help himself. The urge to play along with her game, to take what she offered, supplanted all else. "And if I bed you but you do not find us compatible, what then?"

Which would never, ever happen.

If he bedded her, she would be ruined for all other men just as he would be ruined for all other women. He would make certain of it.

She remained calm and poised, as though they discussed something as simple as the snowfall or Christmas pudding. "If we are not compatible, then naturally neither of us would wish to wed the other."

"A novel concept." He squeezed her breast gently, wishing he could feel her hard nipple kissing his palm. "But if I take your innocence, your brother will have my hide. *I* would have my own hide, for that matter. No gentleman would bed a lady without first giving her his protection."

"My body is mine alone to give." Her chin rose, her stubbornness on display. Damn if it didn't make him want her more. "It is not for you, for my brother, or for anyone else to decide what I choose to do with it. If I am to be bound to a man for the rest of my life, then I need to be sure he is the man I want."

Harry considered Alexandra, drinking in the impressive sight of her. With her copper locks confined in a series of coils and twists and her elegant gown, she looked every inch the part of the lady she was. But she was not the average cossetted miss, and the way she did not shrink from his hand claiming her breast coupled with the boldness of her suggestion confirmed that.

His thumb traced circles over the curve of her breast where he knew her nipple hid. Damn the thickness of her corset for robbing him of the pleasure of torturing it as he longed. But as much as he yearned to take what she offered, he could not find it within him to do so. "I cannot bed you, my lady. It would be wrong."

"It would not be wrong if I wished it," she argued, her tone serious. "If you wished it as well. Society's rules need not define us. I do not know about you, my lord, but I wish for a happy life. Why consign ourselves to a lifetime of misery if it can be avoided?"

She was an innocent. Of that much he was certain now. Only a virgin would assume that one round of fucking could determine whether or not a man and woman were compatible forever. "I do not wish to discourage you from your current path as it would please me more than you know, but one bedding is not enough to determine a lifetime's worth of compatibility."

But Lady Alexandra did not waver in her determination. "It may not be foolproof, but it is what I require. What do you say, Lord Harry? Will you conduct this experiment with me, or do I need to find a substitute?"

The very notion of another man touching her made him want to commit murder. He would tear any other poor sod who got within a foot of her to bloody pieces. He was not a particularly violent man, but everything in him said that he would not share Lady Alexandra Danvers.

"No one else will touch you," he growled, his fingers tightening over her breast as if to stake his claim. For that was how he felt about her, he realized in a moment of stark, shocking realization. Somehow, she had become his. And he would be hers. "I alone will conduct this and all future experiments with you. Is that clear, Alexandra?"

She pursed her lips, considering him in a fashion that could not help but to make him feel as if she saw far more than he would have preferred. "If I desire it."

"Oh you will desire it, my lady." He would make certain of that.

His brother may have snared the lady he had once wished to wed, but Harry was more than competent at seduction. Besides, he had already become convinced that Spencer and Bo were perfect for each other.

Perhaps, whispered a voice inside him before he could stifle its unwanted insight, *Lady Alexandra is perfect for you in the same fashion.*

"You have yet to complete the first experiment," she pointed out then. "How can you be so confident?"

Devil take it. He was left with no other choice. The saucy wench had provoked him, had taken it too far. There was nothing to do but lower his mouth to hers and kiss her as he'd been longing to do from the moment he'd entered the chamber.

Her lips opened in a soft exhalation of surprise, and he took the opportunity to taste her once again as he had in the carriage, sliding his tongue inside the warm cavern of her mouth. This time, she tasted of mulled cider and Christmas and spicy, delicious woman. Her tongue slid against his, tentatively at first but then with greater urgency, her lips clinging to his. She had learned how to kiss him back, what he liked.

And what he liked was ferocity. Brazenness. Uninhibited want. The fantasy of a proper lady who liked to be stripped and fucked made him so hard he lost the capacity to think. He had done his best to quell his wicked longings, knowing they were wrong. But here in the charmed safety of the old north tower, snow blanketing the land, an enchanted season upon them, this eccentric, intriguing woman so soft and lush against him...

He could not do anything but kiss her.

By the grace of God, her arms twined about his neck, bringing him closer to her yet, and her fingers sank into his hair, the soft score of her nails on his scalp telling him she could be as brazen as her suggestion to "experiment" was. Lord Harry Marlow, treasured MP of the Liberal party with his sterling reputation as the faultless younger son of the Duke of Bainbridge, ought not to be dallying with the innocent sister of the Earl of Ravenscroft. Doing so was wrong, and it went against his every principle.

But in the battle of conscience versus lust, his raging desire and painfully hard cockstand were making it clear who the victor would be.

And it wasn't his honor.

Besides, he reminded his protesting conscience, he had already acquired a marriage license. They could wed on the morrow or that very evening before dinner if they chose. To hell with it.

He kissed her harder, with an almost bruising intensity, part of him wondering if she would retreat and part of him needing to brand her in his own way. He kissed her with an abandon he had never experienced with anyone else. He had always viewed gentlewomen as untouchable. They were delicate, rare creatures who were to be treated with kid gloves.

His inner debauchery had longed for him to do more, but he had never allowed it to happen until his moment of weakness in the carriage with Alexandra. Kisses, caresses, tongues, fingers, pleasure, and mindless fucking were all relegated to the sphere of the mistress, as was proper. Lord knew his father the sainted duke had all but embossed that mantra upon his skull.

And yet now, as he breathed in the delicate scent of Lady Alexandra, as he ravaged her mouth with kisses and drank in the sweet, breathy sounds of her pleasure, he could not help but wonder if his father had been wrong. If *he* had been wrong to live a life of duty and observance rather than pursuing what he truly wanted.

Why could he not pleasure the woman he intended to make his wife? If she desired it as much as he, where was the sin? He caught Alexandra's full lower lip in his teeth and tugged, biting before he soothed the sting with a kiss and reared back, studying her.

Her lovely face was flushed, her mouth swollen and berry-red, her blue eyes brilliant. He captured her face in his hands, admiring her as he stroked her jaw with his thumbs. Her skin was soft as satin. He wanted to lick it, to discover what she tasted like everywhere. "You are so bloody beautiful it hurts, Lady Alexandra Danvers."

She stared at him, searching his gaze, almost as if she expected to detect a lie, shaking her head slowly. "I am not beautiful."

"You're gorgeous," he corrected, kissing her again before forcing himself to slow down and disengage once more. "This *experiment* notion of yours. Are you serious about it?"

She nodded without hesitation. "Observation and experiment are the hallmarks of science. One cannot reach an informed conclusion without them."

Science.

He ground his jaw. "To hell with science. This is about you and me, about emotions and needs and wants. Do you want me?"

He needn't ask. Harry recognized the signs, being neither blind nor innocent. But he wanted there to be no question. His honor demanded that if he staked his claim upon her this day, she alone made the decision.

Her gaze went wide. "I...yes. I would very much like to conduct this experiment with you, my lord, above all others."

He wasn't certain if he should be insulted or amused that she continued to refer to the prospect of him bedding her as an experiment. Being a liberal-minded man, he decided upon the former.

"Good." He kissed her once, twice. Three times because he couldn't help himself. She tasted so bloody good, and her lips were too sweet. "I want you too."

Another kiss, then another. His mind spun, plotting the logistics of this sudden assignation. He was a planner by nature, organized and methodical. There wasn't a bed in the north tower room, but there was an accommodating, soft fur rug. The thought of Alexandra laid bare upon it like a pagan sacrifice, her creamy curves, long legs, and pink nipples on display, made his ballocks tighten.

He broke the kisses before he embarrassed himself by spending in his trousers.

"You want me?" Her voice was tentative and adorably befuddled. She blinked at him, eyes wide, as though lost in a dream.

"Mmm." He trailed his touch down her throat, seeking buttons in the pleats and lace adorning the front of her bodice and finding only fabric. "Where are the fastenings?"

Her copper brows rose, swollen lips parting. "On the back of the gown."

"You should have worn the trousers," he growled, losing no time at all in finding the hidden moorings running in an inconvenient line down her spine. "They would have been far simpler to remove."

Another blink. In the circle of his embrace, she held herself as still as a doe in the wood that had just scented a hunter waiting for her to wander within the range of his arrow. "My brother reclaimed them."

"The devil." He frowned, concentrating on the pretty bow of her upper lip as he worked his way down, leaving gaping fabric in his wake. "When we are wed, I'm going to buy you at least a dozen pair."

Her breath caught when he reached the final hook and her gown parted. She shivered.

His thoughts instantly went to her comfort. "Are you cold, sweet?"

She shook her head, her gaze never wavering from his. "No, my lord. Your fingers grazed my skin, and the oddest sensation careened through me."

Lord. Had he made her wet by his mere touch? He could not wait to find out.

"Desire," he clipped, attempting to keep a sharp rein upon his raging lust. "It is called desire."

"Yes." She swallowed, her gaze lowering to his mouth. "I suppose that must be the word for it. If I am to conduct this experiment with proper care, I ought to know the lexicon."

For some reason, Alexandra's continued references to her scientific pursuits made a swift bolt of lust pound through him. She was enchanting and so very rare in her lack of affectation. But the desire to undo her surged, reckless and eager within him.

"If you wish to know the lexicon, let us begin here." He dragged her gown to her waist and freed her arms from the sleeves before taking her hand in his and pressing it to the part of him that longed for her attention the most. "Cock."

"Oh." If possible, those copper-lash-studded eyes went

wider.

"Say it," he commanded, guiding her fingers over him.

"Cock," she whispered.

Holy hell. He was trapped in a fantasy of his own making. Or of her making. It little mattered. All that did matter was that she sat before him in her chemise and corset, her full breasts cinched into an erotic offering, her fingers studiously exploring the length of his engorged prick.

She gripped him, and the breath hissed from his lungs.

Alexandra released him and jerked away, startled. Apologetic. "Oh dear. Did I do something wrong?"

"You did everything right." He ground his jaw and fought once more for control. He began reciting parliamentary bills in his head. There. That quelled the ardor a bit. Not enough, damn it all. "I want to go slowly, however. To take my time and make certain that you find your pleasure."

"Pleasure," she repeated slowly. "What has that to do with sexual congress?"

He almost swallowed his tongue. "Good Lord, woman. It has everything to do with it. Come, let me show you."

Clasping her hands in his, he stood, drawing her to her feet as well. The book she had been reading fell from its abandoned nest beneath her skirts. He wouldn't have noted it but for the fact that it hit him square on the toe and flipped open. He glanced down, and the tinted illustration upon the page at his feet made him pause.

"Is that…"

"Nothing!" her startled exclamation rang through the stone walls of the tower room, echoing. "It is nothing." She nudged the book with the tip of her shoe, snapping it closed.

But not before he had seen the undeniable image of a man on his knees before a woman's spread legs, his head bowed to feast upon her cunny. Shock mingled with a fresh assault of arousal. Had Alexandra been reading a bawdy book, poring over the licentious illustrations? Had she been thinking of him? He had to know.

"I wouldn't refer to your reading material as nothing, sweet." His lips twitched. "I would call it quite edifying."

Her chin raised. "I was conducting research, if you must know."

"Precisely," he agreed, the smirk he'd been attempting to suppress curving his lips at last. "Edifying. What did you learn?"

Her cheeks flamed. She tried to wrest her hands from his grip, but he held firm. "Precious little, I'm afraid. I had only just begun when you interrupted me. Do you wish to continue with our experiment or not, my lord?"

"Harry." Leaving the illicit volume where it lay, he moved toward the fur pelt, tugging her along with him. "Come with me. Where did you come by your naughty book, sweet?"

"A friend."

He stopped and turned back, an unfamiliar, unwelcome spear of jealousy striking his gut. Harry frowned down at her, their hands still entwined. "A male friend?"

"A female friend," she grumbled, her flush heightening until she was red straight to the roots of her glorious hair. "None of your concern."

"Boadicea," he guessed, and he supposed he ought not to have been shocked, but he nevertheless was.

He knew his brother's wife was a rebellious spirit, but he had not realized they shared an interest in the prurient. He owned a rare copy of the illegal, bawdy book that Alexandra had been reading as well. Here was further proof that gently bred ladies were capable of passion and curiosity just as surely as any gentleman. How intriguing.

And how bloody arousing.

"I will not divulge the name of the friend to whom the book belongs," Alexandra chided. "Do not ask it of me."

She was embarrassed. But she need not be. He found the notion of her viewing the wicked images and reading the forbidden, erotic stories within the pages of that leather-bound volume more enticing than he could possibly express.

"Come," was all he said once more, gently tugging her toward the fur. A fire crackled merrily in the grate. Snow fell once again outside, flurrying and settling upon the existing skiff from his inglorious arrival.

She followed him, her fingers tight over his, her dress half-removed, and she was so damn alluring that when he stopped on the cushion of the fur rug, he stilled and simply drank her in. He wanted to do everything to her. To own her. To fuck her. To make her come so hard she saw stars.

The ferocity of his feelings for her shook him to his core. He had never felt this way for another woman. Lady Alexandra Danvers and her fiery hair and unique ways, with her unabashed intelligence and curiosity, affected him as no one else had.

"Alexandra." Her name was torn from him as he stared down at her. "Forget about science and experiments. Is this what you want? Truly what you want? Because after I fuck you, I am going to marry you, and after I marry you, I am going to spend the rest of my days making you want me the way I want you."

Her hands crept to his face, tentatively cupping his jaw, as if she were afraid of his sudden defection. "You want me?"

Her gentle touch, warm and soft, undid did. He stared at her, knowing it was impossible to feel such a strong pull to her after a mere week of courting and yet also knowing that it was undeniably, irrevocably true.

And he needed more.

He needed Alexandra Danvers, naked and beneath him. But he would settle for her any way he could have her. However she wanted him. Whatever she wished.

"Shall our experiment continue?" he asked, need for her making his voice rough.

"Of course." She removed her hands from his face and he would have protested the loss of her touch but for her next action.

She gripped the waist of her dress, pulling it down her full, delicious hips. The silk and lace fell in a soft sigh to pool around her feet in a luxurious heap. Or maybe it was him that sighed. All he knew was that she stood before him in nothing more than her undergarments and he had lost the ability to form a coherent sentence. Chemise, corset, drawers. Ivory eyelet, pink ribbon, feminine frills, and a body that any courtesan would sell her soul to own.

Good. Bloody. Hell.

Words could not dare to define the lush, potent lure of her. He wanted more. Wanted everything. His cock was hard. His mouth was dry. His heart was full. His hands trembled.

He touched her, palms finding the sweet curve of her waist as if it was where they belonged. Her heat swept through the layers keeping him from her skin. She was warm and supple. And he couldn't resist tugging her into his chest and sealing his lips to hers yet again.

A sound of pleasure purred from her throat, and she opened for him at once, her tongue growing bold enough to slip inside his mouth first. In that moment, he forgot they were at a house party. Forgot that they had yet to wed. Forgot that he was about to go against every shred of honor he possessed.

Forgot everything but her and the roaring, raging need to make her his. He deepened the kiss, groaning with his own pent-up lust, and swept a caress from her waist to the neat knot of corset laces at her lower back. His mistresses had always kept their knots loose, ready to release with a simple tug. He realized now that they had dressed with great regard for their occupation.

Lady Alexandra's knot did not release with such ease. Hers, tied by her lady's maid, had been pulled taut with the intent to keep it in place until the evening necessitated the change to her dinner gown. A growl tore from his throat as his one-handed fumbling only seemed to make the dratted thing go tighter.

Alexandra tipped her head back, studying him from beneath the veil of her extravagant lashes, her red, lovely lips pursed. "What is wrong, my lord?"

"Harry," he reminded her again. "No formality in the bedchamber."

"This is not a bedchamber," she pointed out, no doubt driven by her dedication to factual integrity.

Theirs would not be a boring marriage. Expectation sizzled in his gut, spreading through him with the slow, steady lick of a flame about to turn into a conflagration. "Please me, sweet. Say my name."

Her gaze burned into his, and for a moment he thought she would resist just to bedevil him. But then she capitulated. "Harry."

He kissed her, swift and deep, because he couldn't resist. When he broke away, they were both breathless. "You've made an excellent pupil thus far. Now turn about so that I can get this infernal contraption off you."

Trousers and shirts for her in private, he decided. Nothing but. Suddenly, the urge to see her in one of his shirts struck him. *Oh yes.* Alexandra with her hair unbound, skin rosy from a thorough fucking, wearing nothing but one of the crisp, white shirts that he wore beneath his robes for parliamentary debates. How sinfully divine.

But now was not the time for frenzied imaginings when his fantasy had come to life before him.

She did as he asked, presenting him with her back. He took a moment to admire the sleek curve of her neck, the soft hollow between her shoulder blades, the nip of her waist, and the fullness of her rounded bottom. He tugged the knot. It came undone, and he plucked the laces with his index finger, loosening them all the way to the top.

He stepped nearer to her, settling his rigid cock into the welcoming cleft of her backside, and wrapping his arms around her so that he could undo each hook-and-eye fastening on the front of her corset. A row of twelve of the little devils. Finally, the last one opened and he cast the stiffly boned undergarment to the floor.

His hands began a decadent examination. He cupped her breasts, pressed his mouth to the side of her throat. He found her nipples, rolling over the pebbled little nubs with his thumbs. "Your nipples are hard, sweet."

"Oh." She arched her back, grinding her bottom more firmly against his erection and filling his palms with her at the same time. "How strange. They are ordinarily soft."

He bit his lip, willing himself to take this slowly, to savor the moment even as the ravenous beast within him wanted to press her to all fours on the rug, flip up her chemise, and slide home inside her pussy through the slit in her drawers. Her innocence coupled with her unashamed arousal drove him to distraction.

She moved against his cock, as if in invitation. He pinched her nipples in warning. "Stay still, or this experiment will be over before it's even begun."

"Mmm," said the minx. "Would you mind doing that

again? How odd that such a thing should be pleasant. I need to be certain."

She needed to be certain that she liked having her nipples pinched? That did it. He was marrying this woman tonight. They weren't leaving the bedchamber until some time in the new year. Possibly not ever.

He pinched again, not hard enough to bring pain but enough for the sort of wicked pleasure she seemed to enjoy. Another trill sounded in her throat. He absorbed the vibration through his lips as he kissed her creamy skin once more. "How was that?"

"Quite good." She caught his hands in hers, covering them. "But I was wondering…"

"You were wondering?" He found the hollow behind her ear and tongued it.

She guided his hands inside her chemise, and suddenly hot, sleek flesh met his hands instead of fabric. "I was wondering for the purpose of the experiment whether or not the experience would be better without a barrier of cloth."

He licked her again, gently bit her fleshy lobe. "Hell yes it is better without the barrier." Harry gave her nipples another tweak.

She jerked. He thrust his hips.

"Very much so," she said on a lusty sigh. "Yes indeed, I think the experiment must proceed with both of us removing our remaining garments."

The cheeky woman.

She had been fashioned for him. Serious and scholarly, eccentric and bold, yet curious and uninhibited in her passions once they had been awakened. Too bloody good to be true.

"I do believe you are correct," he agreed, reluctantly removing his hands from her luscious breasts and taking a step back. "Take off your chemise and drawers and let down your hair for me."

He was being domineering, he knew, but he wanted to set the pace. In the bedchamber, he preferred to dominate. And he felt, for the first time, that he could truly be himself with Alexandra. That she, with her open, giving heart and her own peculiarities, would accept him as he was.

He shucked his jacket, waistcoat, shirt, shoes, trousers, and smalls. Not even the chill winter's air emanating from the old tower walls could cool his heated skin. He was on fire for her, fully nude, and more aroused than he'd ever been.

He watched as she pulled her chemise over her head and unbuttoned her drawers before allowing them to fall around her ankles. The elegant sweep of her back entranced him, but her rump's full curves were what captured his attention the most. My God, she was beautiful. He wanted to fall to his knees and bite one of those lovely, cream-smooth cheeks.

He swallowed, fighting back another swift, powerful surge of arousal. When she moved to undo her intricate coiffure, he found his wits and stepped forward, staying her. He had changed his mind.

"Allow me."

She stilled, lowering her hands. He had never before lowered a lover's tresses. Had never been struck by the urge. But Alexandra's hair was magnificent. He had always been drawn to ginger-haired women. No other shade of red could compare to her copper locks, which were a delectable strawberry with flaxen highlights that glinted in the sun rays that filtered through the large tower windows. His fingers sank into the soft strands, finding pins and pulling them out one by one. They rained to the floor, some hitting the fur, others landing upon the stone floor with a *plink*.

He unwound braids and coils, amazed at how much of it

there was and how well her lady's maid had trapped the bounty. Alexandra's hair, unbound, was wild and breathtaking. It matched her perfectly. He smoothed it down over her back, his palm stopping at the ends, which reached all the way to the curve of her arse. He sifted through the strands, finding bare, pliable flesh, and filled his hands with her.

She gasped, shooting him a look over her shoulder that was part shocked, part aroused. "My lord?"

He leaned forward, caught her lips with his to reassure her. "You have a tempting bottom." He squeezed gently. "But if you insist upon my lording me, I'm going to spank it."

Up went her finely arched brows. "You wouldn't dare, my lord."

With his right hand, he delivered a painless tap to her rump. "Do you risk testing me?"

He kissed her again, slid his hands over soft, yielding flesh to anchor her waist. Their tongues dueled. He bit the fullness of her lower lip, licked the bow that taunted him each time he gazed upon her. Kissing her from this angle, his body behind hers, her face tilted toward him, his cock grinding against her backside, the silken curtain of her hair whispering over his chest, only served to heighten the sensations licking through him like low, molten flames.

"Harry," she whispered into his mouth. And then she turned in his arms, cupping his face as she had earlier, as though he were someone precious to her. As if he were someone to be cherished. Her tenderness as she stood vulnerable, innocent, and nude before him rocked him to his core.

Something warm slid into place deep in his heart.

Something right.

It wasn't the Christmas season. Or the cold. Or the snow. Or the fantasy of their little bower away from everyone else. It was the woman before him. She was his other half, the piece of himself he had never known was missing until this moment of stark revelation and utter want.

He had fallen in love with Lady Alexandra Danvers.

"Yes, darling." He planted kisses on her cheek, her ear, her chin and jaw. Any speck of skin his lips could find. Her throat, the madly throbbing pulse of her heart. Lower still, all the way to the generous swells of her breasts, at last upon full, erotic display. He kissed his way to the taut bud of one erect nipple and then sucked it into his mouth. "Mmm."

She hummed her pleasure. He licked and bit before moving to the other perfectly pink peak and trailing his tongue in a teasing ring. He kissed below, then above it before straightening, denying her what she so clearly wanted.

"Harry," she said again.

But he had something better in mind. Ignoring her plea, he guided her to her back on the soft fur, taking care to see that she was comfortably settled. He stopped for a beat to take in the full effect of her long, deliciously curved body spread before him like a nude feminine feast before he kissed the peak of her breast. "The next part of the experiment involves communication."

"Please do it again," she said immediately.

He smiled against her skin before kissing to the left of her hungry nipple. She was a quick study, his future wife. "Do what again?" he asked, being deliberately obtuse.

Harry glanced up to find her watching him, her lip caught between her teeth, an adorable flush staining her cheekbones. A quick study, but still an innocent. Never mind that, he would rectify it with great pleasure. And he would also make her tell him exactly what she wanted him to do to her. If she wanted to conduct an experiment, he would damn well give her a bloody experiment. He blew on her nipple.

She gasped and arched her back, thrusting her breast toward him in a wordless plea.

But he would not falter. He kissed the valley between her breasts. Here, she smelled of her soap. Bergamot and orange and sweet, bare woman. "Tell me, Alexandra."

"What you did before," she said on a rush, frustration tingeing her tone.

He blew on the beckoning bud again. "More specific, sweet. I am afraid that I must conduct this experiment with a great deal of attention toward specificity. That way, when we review it, there can be no question of what occurred. Nor will there be any confusion regarding our compatibility."

She made a sound of exasperation. Her fingers threaded through his hair, and she attempted to urge his head toward her waiting nipple. He resisted, prolonging their battle of wills to heighten the passion for both of them. Even if it all but killed him to control his urge to fuck her into the next century as he so desperately longed to do.

"Suck my nipple into your mouth as you did before," she elaborated, her voice strained with need. "And…use your teeth again, if you please."

He had uncovered her libidinous side, and he loved it. "As you wish, sweet. All in the name of our experiment, naturally."

And then he suckled her. Caught her nipple between his teeth and tugged. Licked it. Kissed it. Bit it once more. He held his weight on one forearm as he visited this sensual torture upon her, and his free hand found its home. His fingers parted her slit, encountering hot, slick flesh. He sought her pearl, circling the sensitive nub. Her hips bucked. With two fingers, he worked her, sucking at the same time.

More wetness coated his fingers. His entire body was alive and aflame, his senses filled with her, breathing her in, aware of her every sound and breath and movement. He could not get enough of this. Of her. And the notion that he would be able to spend the rest of his life bringing her pleasure and loving her nearly split him in two.

Too good to be true.

She was.

It was.

They were.

"This experiment is proceeding…" she gasped when his fingers found the particularly sensitive underside of her clitoris at the same time as he bit her. "Oh. That is to say, I am pleased with the experiment thus far. *Harry.*"

He raked her flesh with his teeth and applied more pressure to her pearl. He sucked her nipple and let it fall from his lips with a lusty pop before looking up to meet her gaze as he continued to play within her wet folds. "Pearl." He stroked it lovingly. She was soaking wet. "Also known as gem. Or, more scientifically as clitoris." At the last, he worked it from side to side, applying all his efforts to stimulating her and readying her for the culmination of their experiment.

The rending of her maidenhead.

He did not like to think of it, for he had never taken a virgin. His only lovers had been well-experienced and eager, either for the pleasure he could give them or the coin. Neither had mattered to him. All that had was his ability to slake his needs within their willing flesh.

He wished he had never known another woman before Alexandra, that he could come to her the same way she came to him, innocent and ready for an awakening. They could have discovered their pleasure together. But he was not an untried youth, and he could not undo what had already been done.

All he could do was make certain that she was the only

woman he would ever pleasure again. The only woman he would ever love.

"Pearl," she repeated, her hips thrusting into his in a parody of lovemaking.

She wanted more. The wetness on his fingers suggested she was ready for it. But first, he wanted to taste her. Perhaps it was not the sort of thing one ought to attempt with an inexperienced lady. But the woman he was hellbent upon pleasuring was no ordinary lady. She was Lady Alexandra Danvers, and she did not flinch at stealing her brother's attire and donning it so that she could proceed with her meteorological studies. She was an original.

She was his.

Forever.

Chapter Ten

*L*ORD HARRY—*HARRY*—SUCKLED HER nipple. Alexandra suppressed an indecent moan at the pleasure he inflicted upon her. She had intended this experiment to be methodical. Reasonable. She had somehow anticipated a clear, calm outcome. A list of observations.

But making love with a man had nothing at all to do with science.

And making love with Lord Henry Marlow was not an experiment at all but rather an experience to revel in. If she had ever imagined she could form a logical thought or conduct herself with reason and scientific clarity where he was concerned, she considered herself horribly, ridiculously wrong.

He kissed his way down her belly, and while her inner sense of modesty told her to avert her gaze, she could not stare anywhere but at him. He kissed the jut of her hip bone. His hands bracketed her thighs before sliding inward, urging her to part them. He kissed her mound as his hands spread her legs wide to accommodate...

Oh. My. Heavens.

His mouth.

The first touch of his tongue upon her pearl, as he had instructed her to call it, made her cry out. He circled the sensitive nub of flesh, then flattened his tongue and worked her. Desire swirled.

He licked, traveling along her seam and then delving deeper. Harry sucked her pearl the same way he had sucked her nipples, and she could not control her body's wanton reaction to such splendor. She had thought there could be no greater pleasure than his lips upon hers, but how wrong she'd been. For this, his wicked mouth between her legs, was a whole new level of bliss.

When he used his teeth upon her, she cried out, the pleasure so intense that she thought it would break her. And it almost did, for one more nip of her pearl followed by a slow and steady suck, and her body shook as a wave of ecstasy unlike anything she'd ever known crashed over her.

His tongue worked her until the last, small tremor subsided, and she lay beneath him feeling both boneless and mindless. Harry rose above her, his lips glistening with her juices, his green eyes dark and glittering. "That is called spending, and I plan to make you do it thoroughly and often when we are wed."

Alexandra could not argue with that. "I will hold you to that promise."

He grinned down at her, so handsome that she ached. "Is that a yes, sweet?"

It was an irrefutable yes to everything and anything he wished to do to her.

But as her eyes devoured his form—the strong, broad chest, lean waist ribbed with muscle, strong forearms, and the thick, long rod of his cock—she couldn't resist teasing him. "Yes to which question?"

"To marrying me, minx." He guided her thighs apart and lowered his beautiful body to hers, the head of him brushing over her clitoris. He bowed his head and sucked her nipple. His fingers dipped between them to work her in a delightful new way.

She could not withhold her low, pleased moan of acquiescence, for he knew how to pleasure her far too well. "Oh yes. But in the interest of science, I do think our experiment might continue."

He kissed a path of fire up her throat. "I couldn't agree more."

And then he took her mouth with his in a kiss that was hot, open, and hungry. She tasted the musk of herself on his lips and tongue, and instead of shocking her, it only aroused her more. That same knot of need grew within her, the flesh he had awakened needy and slick. She ached to be filled. To become one with him.

He moved, his cock poised at her opening. She bucked, knowing what she wanted. His fingers played over her pearl.

"Are you certain, Alexandra?" he whispered, kissing her as if she were something to be savored.

"Yes." She rocked again, bringing the tip of him closer still. "I want you inside me."

With one shallow thrust, he broke past the barrier of her maidenhead. A sharp, stinging pain pierced her, but she knew enough to expect it, and she had been prepared. He stilled, tore his lips away, and pressed his forehead to hers. "Did I hurt you, darling?"

He toyed with her pearl more firmly, chasing away the pain with a fresh onslaught of desire. Her hips tipped upward of their own accord, her internal muscles squeezing to bring him deeper. Nothing had ever felt so real or so right. They were joined, connected.

The words spilled forth from her. She could no longer contain them. They were larger than she was. "I love you."

On a groan, he thrust into her until he was fully seated. She was gloriously full and surrounded by him. The weight of his body atop hers, the sensation of him inside her, the heat and scent of skin…it was too much. She never wanted it to end.

He moved then, thrusting in a delicious rhythm. In and out, in and out. Deep then shallow, his skilled fingers never leaving her. Pleasure crashed through her with the force of a runaway locomotive. She tightened around his driving cock as he sank deep inside her, and she screamed her release.

He was not far behind. He thrust again and again as she shuddered and quaked and spent. And then his body stiffened and tensed beneath her questing touch. He slammed home, whispering her name into her mouth as the warm, wet rush of his seed spurted inside her.

He collapsed atop her, his heart thudding to match hers, and kissed her nose. "I love you too, sweet. I have already acquired a license, and we can be married as soon as you wish."

She hugged him to her, burying her face in the delicious heat of his neck. "I have every intention of conducting similar experiments with you as soon as possible. Will tomorrow do?"

The rumble of his laughter and the sweetness of another kiss rewarded her. "You are an utter gem, Danvers. Who could have known my Christmas angel would come to me in the middle of an Oxfordshire blizzard, wearing her brother's clothes?"

Alexandra kissed him again, for she couldn't seem to help herself. "Did you mean what you said about the trousers?"

A sinful smile curved his sensual lips. "I meant what I said about everything, sweet. You appeared in my life when I least expected it, but when I needed you most. I love you exactly as you are. You're perfection."

"I love you Harry Archibald Marlow." Happiness suffused her, mingling with the delicious glow that had flooded her in the wake of their lovemaking. "And I also meant what I said about marrying you tomorrow."

He laughed and kissed her again. "Consider it done, my love."

Epilogue

Six months later

THE WEATHER WAS insufferably warm, and there was a thunderstorm rolling in, making the conditions perfect for studying the clouds in an effort to complete, at last, her weather prognostics map. Alexandra noted the reading from the barometer in her journal before holding her spectroscope to her eye and observing the striations of the clouds. Here, at last, she was certain, was the missing pieces in her research.

It had only taken her six months, one wedding, and one indefinably wonderful husband to reach her final conclusions. She made some more notes in her journal, sketching out the bands of the spectrum, beginning at left with red, then carrying on to orange, yellow, green and finally ending at right with blue.

By the time she had completed her notations, ominous cracks of thunder could be heard, trembling on the horizon. Lightning bolts arced across the sky, traveling between clouds. For a moment, she stood in awe, watching the beauty of the storm. The air was redolent with the scent of imminent rain.

Nature was fierce and incredible.

A strong arm wrapped around her waist, and the voice she had come to know and love so well, butter smooth and every bit as rich and decadent, murmured in her ear. "Have you finished taking your notes, my love? I fear lingering here much longer will not be safe."

Alexandra turned to a sight even more fierce and incredible than the impending storm: her handsome husband. Looping her arms around his neck, she drew his mouth down to hers for a kiss that began as sweet and innocent and soon turned into a hungry, frenzied meeting of lips and tongue and teeth.

With a growl, he held her tighter, angling his mouth over hers and exerting just the right amount of pressure before catching her lower lip in his teeth and giving her a tender nip. "I love you," she said on a contented sigh, rubbing her nose against his.

She could not seem to stop telling him, now that he had unlocked that part of herself. And even though it seemed hardly enough. Three simple, monosyllabic words could not begin to convey the depth of emotion she felt for Harry.

She showed him with her caresses on his body, with her tongue against his. She showed him every night in their bed and even sometimes in his study. And the library. Oh, and there had been that occasion for wickedness in the hall when no one else had been about…

She was flushing, she was certain, her cheeks hot and prickly.

"I love you too, angel." He kissed her again, his eyes blazing with intensity as they burned into hers. "And you are flushing, which leads me to believe you are having indecent thoughts about the carriage awaiting us."

She had not been, but now he mentioned it…

Alexandra could not stifle her smile. "Carriages shall forever hold a fond place in my heart. I seem to recall a very naughty carriage ride with a certain gentleman that changed my life forever."

He grinned back at her, those creases bracketing his eyes

that she had kissed so often appearing. "I remember it well. The snow was falling down like mad, and the loveliest gentleman I've ever seen was standing in the midst of it, studying the snow bands and laughing at me for berating the clouds."

"Ah yes. I think I may know the gentleman you speak of." She could not resist kissing his smiling lips once more. And then again. And then again.

A violent crack of thunder interrupted their reminiscing, reminding them their time was limited and the storm would sweep in all too soon. She quickly extricated herself from his embrace, knowing she needed to gather up her journal and instruments before they returned to the carriage.

A sudden jab to her midsection stilled her. She pressed her hands over the gentle roundness of her belly, hugged by the special trousers and shirt she had commissioned for her scientific expeditions. There was simply something so freeing about moving without the encumbrance of skirts and petticoats, and Harry not only did not mind her eccentricity, but he rather enjoyed the sight of her limbs on display for him.

Harry was before her instantly, his countenance worried. "What is it, darling? Is it the babe?"

"Yes." A new sense of awe burst open inside her, the wonderment of the little life they had created together making itself known. "I do believe he has just kicked me." She took Harry's hand in hers and pressed it over her belly. Another flurry of movement rippled within her, thumping against his splayed palm. "There. Do you feel him?"

"I do." His expression mirrored hers, she was sure: love, reverence, astonishment. "I think she is an incredibly intelligent female just like her mother, and she is telling us to get back into that carriage before the storm unleashes its rage upon our heads."

Tears of happiness filled her eyes, and she had to blink them furiously away so she could see her husband's face once more. "You learned all that from one kick?"

"I did. You see, I too am an intelligent man. That is why I married her mother."

She pursed her lips, her hand still pressed atop his, free of gloves so that they were skin upon skin. "I thought you married her because you thoroughly compromised her in a carriage in the middle of a blizzard."

"No." He shook his head slowly and dipped his head for one more kiss. "I married her because she is the other half of me. Because I cannot be me without her. Because the sight of her in trousers is enough to make me weak in the knees. Because I love her with all my heart, and I cannot wait to get her back to Boswell House so I can make slow and sweet love to her."

"Will you be on your knees?" she asked, feeling impish.

Thunder cracked again as lightning flashed in the distance.

"For you, always." He released her and made short work of collecting her implements, journal, and the small folding table she had brought along for her studies. Holding it beneath one arm, he offered her the other. "Our carriage awaits, darling."

She took his arm, holding on tightly and with much gratitude and love. "I have heard all manner of things can happen within a carriage," she teased.

"Only the very best, my love, for look at where it brought us."

"Yes." She accepted his aid into the carriage and seated herself, watching him place her things inside before he joined her on the bench, his arms wrapping around her. "Just look."

As the carriage rocked into motion, Harry sealed his lips over hers, and it was just like that enchanted day in the snow all over again, but this time, there was no scandal awaiting them at the other end of their journey. This time, there was only happiness and a lifetime of love.

Dear Reader,

Thank you for reading *The Night Before Scandal*! I hope you enjoyed this seventh book in the Heart's Temptation series and you loved the return of some of my favorite characters from past books. Harry and Alexandra both deserved their happily ever after, and I was thrilled to give it to them in this special holiday-themed novella.

As always, please consider leaving an honest review of *The Night Before Scandal*. Reviews are greatly appreciated! If you'd like to keep up to date with my latest releases and series news, sign up for my newsletter here (scarlettscottauthor.com/contact) or follow me on Amazon or BookBub. Join my reader's group on Facebook for bonus content, early excerpts, giveaways, and more.

Have you read my other series? If you like your historical romance scorching hot, why not give them a try? Read on for a sample from the first book in the League of Dukes series.

Until next time,

Scarlett

Nobody's Duke
League of Dukes Book One

By
Scarlett Scott

A widow with secrets

When the dangerous men who killed her husband in a political assassination threaten Ara, Duchess of Burghly, the Crown assigns her a bodyguard. But the man charged with protecting her is no stranger.

He's Clayton Ludlow, the bastard son of a duke and the first man she ever loved. Eight years after he took her innocence and ruthlessly abandoned her, he's back in her drawing room and her life.

This time, she's older, wiser, and stronger. She will resist him at any cost and make him pay for the past.

A man with a broken heart

She's the only woman Clay ever loved and the one he hates above all others. When Ara brutally betrayed and deceived him, leaving him with a scarred face and a bitter heart, he devoted himself to earning his reputation as one of the Crown's most feared agents.

He wants nothing more than to finish his assignment so that he can remove all traces of her from his life forever. But walking away from her for good won't be as easy as he thinks.

As secrets are revealed and danger threatens Ara, Clay discovers that the truth is far more complicated than deceit. Once she's back in his arms where she belongs, he'll wage the biggest fight of all to keep her there.

Chapter One

>>>>><<<<<

London, 1882

TO SOCIETY, SHE was the Duchess of Burghly. To her husband, murdered by a Fenian's blade, she had been Araminta, formal and proper and beloved by him in his way. She had loved him equally in her way. Sweet Freddie, with the heart of an angel and the desire to change a world that would never understand or accept him.

She was all too familiar with the way the world treated hopeful, unsullied hearts.

"Ara."

She had been hopeful and unsullied once.

When she had known the man standing before her in the drawing room of Burghly House. When she had loved him. When she had been...

"Ara."

There it was again, spoken with such dark vehemence that it almost vibrated in the air, sending unwanted tendrils of heat licking through her even after all the years that had passed. That name, that bitter reminder of who she had been, spoken in the voice that had once sent a thrill straight to her heart...it was her undoing.

Ara had not realized she had clambered to her feet until her body swayed like a tree caught in an aggressive wind. Faintness overcame her. Her vision darkened. The palms clenching her silken skirts were damp, hands trembling.

He was taller than she remembered. Broader and stronger. He had always been a mountain of a man, but he had grown into his bones and skin, and the result took her breath despite her fierce need to remain as unaffected by him as possible. His eyes, cold and flat, burned into her. His jaw was rigid, his expression blank. A vicious-looking scar cut down his cheek.

She wondered for a moment how he could have received such a mark.

And then she reminded herself that she did not care. That he had ceased to be someone she worried after some eight years ago, on the day she had waited for him with nothing more than a valise and her foolish heart. He had never come.

The agony of that day returned to her a hundredfold as she stood in the gilt splendor of her drawing room, stabbing at her with the precision of a blade. Hours had passed, day bleeding into evening, and she had waited and waited. The only carriage to arrive had been her father's, and it had taken her, broken and dejected, back to the place from which she had fled.

"Your Grace, are you well?"

The voice of the Duke of Carlisle, edged with concern, pierced her consciousness, reminding her she had an audience, lest she allow her dignity to so diminish that she allowed *him* to see the visceral effect he had upon her.

She swallowed, tamped down the bile threatening to curdle her throat, and turned her attention to Carlisle. "I am as well as can be expected, given the events of the last three months, Duke. I thank you for your concern."

He inclined his head. "I am deeply sorry for the loss of your husband, madam. He was a bright star in the Liberal party."

"Yes," she agreed, a tremor in her voice that she could not

suppress. Speaking of Freddie inevitably festered a resurgence of horror and sadness. He had been a good man, an estimable husband to her and father to Edward, and he had not deserved to die choking on his own blood in a Dublin park. "He was."

Carlisle's lips compressed into a pained frown. "I cannot begin to fathom your grief, and I apologize for our unwanted presence here today. If there were any way to keep you free of this burden, I wholeheartedly would."

"The grief is immense," she whispered, all she could manage past the knot in her throat.

How she hated that it wasn't just her sorrow for Freddie that paralyzed her now and stole her voice. She felt *his* stare upon her like a brand. He had not moved. Had not spoken another word save her name, and yet he seemed to have stolen all the air from the room.

"As I was saying prior to Mr. Ludlow's arrival," Carlisle continued with a formal tone, "it is with great regret that I find myself tasked with informing you that there has been a threat made against you by the same faction of Fenians that murdered your husband. To that end, the Home Office has assigned an agent to ensure your protection."

Carlisle's words sank into her mind as though spoken from a great distance.

…a threat made against you…

…same Fenians that murdered…

…an agent to ensure your protection.

Her breathing was shallow. Her fingers fisted in her skirts with so much force that her knuckles ached. Still, the weight of *his* burning gaze upon her would not lift. Her entire body felt achy and hot and itchy and chaotic all at once.

"Would you care to elaborate on the nature of the threat?" She kept her eyes carefully trained upon the Duke of Carlisle, but it was impossible to keep *him* from her peripheral vision.

He filled the chamber as much with his presence as with his massive size.

The Duke of Carlisle, despite his reputation as a depraved reprobate, was the unexpected liaison between herself and the department of the government responsible for informing her about Freddie's murder and the investigation into finding his assassins. Their previous meetings had been equally stilted, revolving around his sympathy for her loss and any new information regarding the Fenians who had plotted Freddie's death.

In the murky days following her husband's murder, she and Edward had been removed from Dublin with an armed escort, but she had imagined that they had left all danger behind them in Ireland.

"Assassination, Your Grace." Carlisle's tone was quiet but deadly serious.

Those three words, so succinct and cold, struck her heart.

Edward could not lose both his parents in the span of three months. Her heart squeezed at the thought of her son alone in the world. Her beautiful, kindhearted boy. She would do anything to protect him.

Her mouth went dry. "I see." She paused, attempted to collect herself, an odd mixture of discomfit at *his* continued presence and fear swirling through her. "My son, Your Grace? Has he been included in the threats as well, or do they only pertain to myself?"

"Your son was not referenced in the threats, Your Grace," Carlisle said.

"*You have a son?*"

She flinched, the angry lash of *his* voice striking her. Still, she would not look at *him*. "I do not understand the reason for your…associate's presence, Your Grace. Indeed, I would far prefer to conduct this dialogue with you in private, as befitting the sensitive nature of the circumstances."

Ara refused to say *his* name. Refused to even think it. Would not speak aloud the true nature of what and who he was. A bastard. The half brother of the Duke of Carlisle. The man she had lost her heart and her innocence to. Her son's father.

No. Freddie had been Edward's father, the only one he had ever known. And it must—*would*—remain that way until she went to her grave.

The Duke of Carlisle appeared unperturbed by her uncharacteristic outburst. "Pray forgive me again, Duchess, but Mr. Ludlow's presence here today is necessary as he is the agent who has been assigned to your protection."

"No!" The word left her in a cry, torn from her, vehement.

But what surprised her the most was that it was echoed by another voice, dark and deep and haunting in its velvety timbre.

His.

Her gaze flitted back to him, and the stark rage she read reflected in the depths of his brown eyes shook her. Beneath the surface, he was seething.

"I will not guard her under any circumstances, Leo. Find someone else," he sneered. "Anyone else."

And then he turned on his heel and stalked from her drawing room, slamming the door at his back.

> Want more? Read Nobody's Duke
> (League of Dukes Book One)!

Don't miss Scarlett's other romances!

(Listed by Series)

Complete Book List
scarlettscottauthor.com/books

HISTORICAL ROMANCE

Heart's Temptation
A Mad Passion (Book One)
Rebel Love (Book Two)
Reckless Need (Book Three)
Sweet Scandal (Book Four)
Restless Rake (Book Five)
Darling Duke (Book Six)
The Night Before Scandal (Book Seven)

Wicked Husbands
Her Errant Earl (Book One)
Her Lovestruck Lord (Book Two)
Her Reformed Rake (Book Three)
Her Deceptive Duke (Book Four)

League of Dukes
Nobody's Duke (Book One)
Heartless Duke (Book Two)
Dangerous Duke (Book Three)

Sins and Scoundrels
Duke of Depravity (Book One)
Prince of Persuasion (Book Two)

Stand-alone Novella
Lord of Pirates

CONTEMPORARY ROMANCE

Love's Second Chance
Reprieve (Book One)
Perfect Persuasion (Book Two)
Win My Love (Book Three)

Coastal Heat
Loved Up (Book One)

About the Author

Amazon bestselling author Scarlett Scott writes steamy Victorian and Regency romance with strong, intelligent heroines and sexy alpha heroes. She lives in Pennsylvania with her Canadian husband, adorable identical twins, and one TV-loving dog.

A self-professed literary junkie and nerd, she loves reading anything, but especially romance novels, poetry, and Middle English verse. Catch up with her on her website www.scarlettscottauthor.com. Hearing from readers never fails to make her day.

Scarlett's complete book list and information about upcoming releases can be found at www.scarlettscottauthor.com.

Connect with Scarlett! You can find her here:
Join Scarlett Scott's reader's group on Facebook for early excerpts, giveaways, and a whole lot of fun!
Sign up for her newsletter here.
scarlettscottauthor.com/contact
Follow Scarlett on Amazon
Follow Scarlett on BookBub
www.instagram.com/scarlettscottauthor
www.twitter.com/scarscoromance
www.pinterest.com/scarlettscott
www.facebook.com/AuthorScarlettScott
Join the Historical Harlots on Facebook

Printed in Great Britain
by Amazon